A Black Place and a White Place

Wisteria Tearoom Mysteries

A Fatal Twist of Lemon
A Sprig of Blossomed Thorn
An Aria of Omens
A Bodkin for the Bride
A Masquerade of Muertos
As Red as Any Blood
A Black Place and a White Place

Intermezzi (Interludes)

"Intermezzo: Spirit Matters"
(to be read between *A Masquerade of Muertos*
and *As Red as Any Blood*)

"Intermezzo: Family Matters"
(to be read between *As Red as Any Blood*
and *A Black Place and a White Place*)

A BLACK PLACE AND A WHITE PLACE

PATRICE GREENWOOD

Evennight Books/Book View Café
Cedar Crest, New Mexico

This is a work of fiction. All of the characters, organizations, and events portrayed in this novel are either products of the author's imagination or are used fictitiously.

A BLACK PLACE AND A WHITE PLACE

An Evennight Book
Published by Book View Café Publishing Cooperative
P.O. Box 1624
Cedar Crest, NM 87008

www.bookviewcafe.com

Cover photo: Pati Nagle
Map illustrations: Chris Krohn and Patrice Greenwood

ISBN: 978-1-61138-878-7

First Edition January 2020

for Marsha
dear friend and faithful tea buddy
(It's your turn.)

Acknowledgments

My thanks to my wonderful publication team for their help with this novel: Sherwood Smith and Chris Krohn; to my dear friends and patient consultants Ken and Marilyn Dusenberry; and to my colleagues in Book View Café.

And as always, thanks to Mary Alice Higbie and the staff of the St. James Tearoom, a world-class tearoom not to be missed.

"Such a beautiful untouched lonely-feeling place—part of what I call the Far Away."

—Georgia O'Keeffe, on the Black Place

"ARE YOU SURE YOU WANT TO DO MACARONS FOR FEBRUARY?" I asked Julio. "They're so labor-intensive."

Julio refilled his coffee mug from a stainless steel thermos. "Macarons are a signal to our clientele that we're a top-shelf establishment. Any coffee shop can make cookies. Macarons show that we mean business."

I lifted the cozy from my teapot and replenished my tea. "We're bound to be busy around Valentine's, though. Wouldn't another month be easier?"

"This is the tearoom's first Valentine's," Julio replied, his dark eyes holding my gaze. "Don't you want to make people long to come back next year? Try them."

He pushed a small plate toward me. It held a half-dozen miniature macarons: some a blushing pink, some a pale, creamy yellow.

"Raspberry and champagne?" I guessed.

"Raspberry-rose and elderflower."

"Oh, my."

I took a creamy macaron and bit into it. The texture was perfect—classic crispy outside and chewy interior—and I knew from experience that it wasn't easy to get right. Sugar and almond were overlaid with the ethereal floral sweetness of elderflower. I gave in to a sigh of pleasure.

"They're heavenly, Julio." I tried a pink macaron: a bright burst of raspberry up front, followed by the gentler rose flavor. I finished it in two bites, taking time to savor the flavors and decide that they were well-balanced. "Divine. But two florals? Some people don't like them."

"There will be a chocolate macaron as well, with two choices of filling—hazelnut or dark ganache." He smiled slyly. "You don't really want to have Valentines without them, do you?"

"How could I? You win."

Julio grinned. "Thanks."

"Are you going to need a part-timer for February?"

"Maybe. But not because of the macarons. Kris said Valentine's week is booking up already. You may have another sold-out month on your hands."

"Well, at least we'll be able to catch our breath *this* month."

I finished the elderflower macaron and sipped my tea, resisting the temptation to take another. The fire crackled gently in the little kiva fireplace near the break table where Julio and I sat with our notebooks and calendars. We were alone in the kitchen at 7:30 a.m., having our January "first Monday" planning session, which had evolved out of necessity throughout the previous year.

On the first Monday of each month, we reviewed the new menu and discussed strategy not only for the current month, but for the weeks ahead, trying to anticipate any special problems that might arise. It was a rare and pleasant opportunity for me and my chef to chat at length, without the rest of the staff present and therefore without interruptions.

The day was overcast and quiet. Just a few days past New Year's, Santa Fe was recovering from the holidays. While there were still plenty of tourists enjoying skiing and shopping and dining, their numbers were noticeably reduced. The tearoom was well-booked, but not sold out, for the coming week. Julio had created a perfect January menu with an emphasis on cheeses, greens, and fresh fruits—a delightful respite from the heavy holiday fare of the previous month. The fact that we were able to look ahead to February was due to the lighter demands of our bookings for January, so far.

"Anything else up your sleeve for Valentine's?" I asked.

"Nothing you don't know about. Edible rose petals are already ordered."

"OK. Have you thought about March at all?"

"Just playing with ideas at this point. Do you want to do a St.

Patrick's Day theme?"

"Not for the whole month," I said, suppressing a shudder at the idea of a month's worth of corned beef. "Maybe a special event. A harp concert, or something."

Julio nodded. "I think I could put you in touch with some Celtic harpists. Or maybe Ramon can get you a concert harpist."

"Both of those sound good. Let's see what develops."

My teacup was empty again. I refilled it, then glanced up at the sound of a car arriving out back. Julio looked over his shoulder toward the window.

"Sounds like Kris."

He was right. A minute later my office manager came in through the kitchen door, bundled to the neck in a black wool coat, black scarf, black boots—her usual "Goth professional" look. Her black hair was uncovered; she rarely wore hats, even on the coldest days. She came over to the table to greet us.

"Happy New Year, Kris!" I said.

"Happy…New Year. Nice ring," she said, catching my gaze. "Got something to tell us?"

I felt myself blush a little, and sipped my tea to hide it. "Yes, Tony and I are engaged." The words, which I hadn't yet said very often, still made me feel a bit breathless.

Kris's attention wandered to the macarons. "Congrats. Or should I say, 'Best wishes'?"

"I think even Miss Manners would admit it's no longer necessary to refrain from congratulating a bride," I said. "Thank you."

Kris picked up the plate of macarons. "These for February?"

"Yes," Julio said.

"I'll let you know what I think."

She carried them out to the hall, on her way to her office upstairs. This was abrupt even for Kris. She had a Goth's cynicism, but she was generally polite. Her boots clicked briskly on the wood floor in the hall, then were muffled by the carpet on the stairs.

Maybe my engagement had reminded her of her recent loss. Though it seemed long ago, it was only a couple of months since Gabriel's death. Kris had made it clear to me that she hadn't expected that to be a long-term relationship, but neither had she expected it to be cut short.

I looked at Julio, who was watching me.

"I didn't know whether to say anything," he said. "Congratulations."

"Thanks." I sipped my tea. "I guess I should make an announcement to the staff."

"Just tell Rosa and everyone will know within twenty-four hours." Julio poured the last of his coffee into his mug. "Have you set a date?"

"September. We won't have it here, but if you're interested I'd love to have you cater."

"I'm interested. Where will it be?"

"I'm not sure yet. I'm thinking outdoors."

"But not in your garden."

"I don't want to end up working the event."

"Good point. Well, if it's on top of Baldy, it'll be a challenge, but I'll do my best."

I chuckled, glancing toward the window. Outside, though not visible from the kitchen, was Santa Fe Baldy, the mountain to which he'd referred, part of the Sangre de Cristos. "Thanks. I'll try to be less ambitious than that."

We discussed a few more details about January, then I carried my tea tray upstairs while Julio began making scones. I paused in my suite to rinse the pot and my teacup before taking them across the hall to the "office" side.

The samovar the staff had given me for Christmas was hot; I had fired it up when I made my first pot of tea. I took a caddy of Lapsang Souchong out of the chest and set some brewing. The smoky flavor of it was a wake-me-up punch that I usually saved for hectic days, but it was Kris's favorite tea.

While it was steeping, I gazed at the framed O'Keeffe poster on the wall outside Kris's office, one of six Santa Fe Chamber Music posters that I had recently unearthed from storage and hung in the upstairs hall. They had belonged to my mother, and had been objects of my childhood fascination. All of them featured artwork by Georgia O'Keeffe.

On a whim, I had chosen to hang the most Goth-like image, *Black Place III*, outside Kris's office. So far, she hadn't commented.

I never tired of gazing at it: soft, lumpy black and gray hills with touches of sandstone red and pink, white shapes that might be more hills or might be clouds, and a jagged stripe down the middle that could be a river or lightning or a crack opening up in the very earth. Or perhaps just an abstraction. One could probably write a dissertation on the subject.

No doubt someone already had. O'Keeffe was New Mexico's most famous artist, her name still a household word decades after her death. She'd spent her final days in Santa Fe, but her definitive New Mexico home was at Abiquiu.

The tea timer went off. I removed the infuser from the pot, then got out a second cup and saucer and carried it all into Kris's office on the tray.

"Cup of tea?" I said, trying for a tone of gentle brightness.

She glanced at me, gave a short nod, and returned her attention to her computer. I filled her cup and set it at her elbow, noting that the plate of macarons sat untouched nearby, then settled into a guest chair with my own tea.

"How was New Year's?" I asked.

"Fab. We had a black-and-white banquet."

"Oh, yes—but I thought it was going to be a ball?"

"Couldn't get a room big enough. They were all booked up by August. We'll have to start planning earlier this year." Her fingers punched rapidly at her keyboard for a few seconds, then she hit the return button and leaned back, looking at me. "Just as well. A ball would have been a bit much right now."

I nodded in sympathy, then sipped my tea. Kris's gaze followed my hands.

"So when did he pop the question?"

"Christmas Eve," I said.

"Were you expecting it?"

"I don't think *he* was expecting it. It sort of—developed out of our conversation."

Her expression grew skeptical, then she took a pink macaron from the plate. "Well, good luck. You know, cops and marriage...."

"I know. Believe me, Tony knows too. He wants this to work."

"I'm sure he does."

She popped the macaron whole into her mouth and crunched it while she typed some more. I doubted she would notice the delicate flavors of the sweet, eating it like that. I watched her, troubled by what seemed to be an undercurrent of anger in her manner. My earlier theory—that she might be sad or envious of my engagement—didn't seem to fit, so I discarded it. What could be bothering her?

"What are you working on this morning?" I asked.

"W4s and 1099s. Once those are done, I'll start the taxes."

And here I'd thought January would be a slow month. When I'd set up the business last spring, and hired Kris, the first thing she'd advised was that I incorporate. That meant annual reports to be filed, and corporate taxes—matters of mystery to me. I was deeply grateful to have Kris on my team to handle such things. I only wished I could help her into a better mood.

But then, maybe she enjoyed this mood. Maybe it was a Goth thing.

I finished my tea and stood. "Well, I'll stop distracting you. You know where to find me if you need me."

Kris nodded, eyes on the screen, hand reaching for another macaron that I suspected she'd neither see nor taste. I carried the tea tray out and set it beside the samovar, refilled my cup, and covered the pot with a cozy. Since it was a Lapsang Souchong day, I fetched a little jar of sour cherry preserves from my suite and set it on the tray, then added a spoonful to my cup. The sweet and sour tones were a perfect complement to the smoky tea, turning it into a cup of luxury.

At my desk, I poked through the perennial heap of message slips, and turned on my computer to tackle the backlog of email. Half of it was so out of date I didn't even bother responding. To personal messages, I replied personally, if only with a brief note to the effect of "sorry I missed this."

It took me a couple of hours to whittle the inbox down to a reasonable size. I was just about to get up for more tea when I heard a "shave-and-a-haircut" knock on the open door frame of my office.

Nat was standing there, holding a fat paperback book and wearing a furry hat over her winter coat. She grinned at me.

"I'm kidnapping you for lunch," she announced.

"Oh, *thank* you!" I got up, gleefully abandoning the correspondence. "Let me get my purse and a coat."

I poked my head into Kris's office. "You want to come to lunch?"

She shook her head. "No, thanks."

Nat followed me out to the hall and handed me her book at

the door to my suite. "It's a biography of Georgia O'Keeffe. I just finished it. Thought you'd enjoy it." She gestured to the art posters on the walls.

"Thanks! I'll just be a minute."

I put the book in my wing chair, promising myself an hour of *reading* time later. Mondays were supposedly part of my weekends, but I usually wound up working. I grabbed my coat, scarf, and purse, and rejoined Nat in the hall.

She was admiring the print of *From the Faraway Nearby*. "I remember when Geneva was collecting these. She was so excited! She was a huge fan of O'Keeffe."

I nodded. I remembered it too, though I'd been little. Back then, all I knew about O'Keeffe was that she lived up north past Española, and she was a famous painter, and nobody ever saw her.

Hunger nudged me toward the stairs. "Where are we going?"

"Santacafé," Nat said, following me down. "My treat. I made us a reservation."

"Wonderful! I haven't been there in ages."

"I know Julio's roommate works there."

"Ex-roommate. Julio's got a new…place."

"Oh?" Nat said as we reached the ground floor.

Not wanting to talk about Julio where he might hear, I waited until we were outside to continue. Nat walked past her car, and I followed her down my snow-patched driveway. The restaurant was just a few blocks away.

"Julio has a new roommate," I told Nat as we reached the street and turned north. "He moved in November. I thought you knew."

"I was a bit preoccupied in November," Nat said. "Is his friend still at Santacafé?"

"I think so."

My ears were getting chilled by a cold breeze. I wrapped my scarf over my head and strode out. We didn't talk much more until we were inside the old, low-ceilinged adobe building and seated at a tiny table by a fireplace in a back room.

"How's the year going for you so far?" Nat asked as we shed our coats and settled in.

"Great. I goofed off all weekend."

"With Tony?"

"He was working, but we had dinner together."

Actually, Tony had been spending nights with me, though he said he'd sleep at his apartment during the week. My staff couldn't resist knowing glances if they encountered him leaving in the morning, and Tony was a private person.

One more reason why we'd have to find a place to live apart from the tearoom. My suite was too small for both of us, and there were other considerations.

"We went to Ten Thousand Waves," I said. "Thank you for the gift card. It was lovely."

"Oh, good! But I meant for you to get a massage."

"It was better than a massage."

Nat chuckled. "You two should spend a weekend there. This month, while business is slow."

I shook my head. "The lodging is pretty pricey, and I'm sure it's booked up with skiers."

"Well, some other place, then. You haven't had a vacation since you opened the tearoom."

"I know. Yes, you're right."

A waiter appeared and kept us busy for a few minutes, reciting specials and taking our order. When she was gone, Nat returned to the subject.

"I'd be happy to fill in for you at the tearoom for a couple of days. And I'll spring for a room if that will help."

"No, no. You've been so generous. We can afford a room. There are less expensive places."

Our coffees arrived, giving me a moment to think about where to stage a getaway. I *did* like the idea. Tony and I could use some quality time away from work. The trick would be whether he could take time off.

"Holiday weekend coming up," Nat said, as if reading my thoughts.

That could making getting a hotel room more difficult. But it might be more convenient for Tony.

"Have you ever stayed at Ghost Ranch?" I asked.

"Years ago," Nat said. "I used to go up there on retreats with my yoga group. It's a little rustic. The Abiquiu Inn is nicer."

I'd always been intrigued by the name, Ghost Ranch. On family car trips we'd driven past the entrance—a big gate with a cow's skull painted on it—but we'd never stopped. The landscapes up there were amazing, and I knew that Georgia O'Keeffe had painted a lot of them.

"O'Keeffe lived at Ghost Ranch for a while, didn't she?"

"There, and in Abiquiu," Nat said. "That book I gave you tells all about it. She stayed at Ghost Ranch in a guest house, then bought a ranch house on the property from the owner, then later she added the Abiquiu house, because it was easier to get supplies in winter. The ranch house is pretty remote."

I nodded. Our lunch was served, so we dropped the subject in favor of duck crepes and watercress salad. If Andre had anything to do with our meals, I never knew, but everything was delicious.

"So, are you and Manny making plans for Paris?" I asked.

"The Louvre for sure, and Meriage Frères. Maybe Versailles. Manny wants to stand on top of the Eiffel Tower, of course. That's all we know so far."

"Oh! Meriage Frères! Bring me some tea?"

"You bet! I may take a collapsible bag and fill it with tea."

I had a fleeting urge to ask if I could stow away in that bag. Paris was on my bucket list, and the famous Parisian tea purveyor would be number one on my agenda whenever I got there.

Which wouldn't be soon. I wanted to get the mortgage on the tearoom paid down first, and this year was busy enough.

We lingered over dessert, and had a pleasant walk back to the tearoom with the wind at our backs. The sun was playing peek-a-boo through clouds that were breaking up a bit now.

Nat saw me to the back door of the house. "You don't need me this week?"

"No, no. Enjoy your freedom."

"You, too, dear. Enjoy that book."

"I will."

I checked in on the kitchen before going upstairs. Hanh had joined Julio, and together they were cranking out scones. They were an efficient team. They'd soon have enough for the whole week.

"Happy New Year, Hanh," I said.

She nodded briskly, sending a ripple down her long, black ponytail. Eyes on her work, she pressed the cutter cleanly straight down through the dough. "Happy New Year."

I started to go, then turned back. "Hanh, do you celebrate a different New Year?"

She paused, looking up at me in mild surprise. "Tet," she said.

I remained unenlightened. "Is that anything like Chinese New Year?"

"Some years it's the same day. Some years a little different. It's calculated differently."

"Ah," I said. "I didn't know about it. Thank you."

As I climbed the stairs, I mused about Vietnamese culture, of which I knew pretty much nothing. Hanh was a great cook. Maybe she and Julio could look at doing a Vietnamese menu some time? Or even just a food item or two...

Kris had deposited some paperwork on my desk, so it was almost an hour before I could slip away to my suite and read for a bit. I'd had enough Lapsang Souchong for one day. I brewed myself a pot of Darjeeling and peeled a clementine, then settled into my wing chair and opened the O'Keeffe biography.

I was soon engrossed. The author had done her homework, referring to newspaper social columns and personal correspondence of the O'Keeffe family, their friends, and their acquaintances. The portrait that emerged was of a no-nonsense child from a Midwestern family, who had decided early on and for inexplicable reasons that she would be an artist, and had held to that choice, tenuously at first, and before long with single-minded determination.

In the early twentieth century, art (like most professions) was dominated by men. O'Keeffe's chances of success were not high, and as her family's prosperity dwindled, they became ever slimmer. Yet she only grew more focused on her chosen path.

Having studied and enjoyed the arts myself, I understood her need for uncompromising focus. I would have liked to be a professional musician, but knowing how difficult it would be to earn a living, I had abandoned that dream.

O'Keeffe, on the other hand, had clung to her dream with an iron will, cutting away everything that did not serve her goal. She adopted an austere lifestyle. She almost always wore black, as if color in her clothing would distract her from the colors that were her tools. She kept nothing extraneous to survival, with the exception of art supplies. She spent her hard-earned pennies on the best materials available for her craft, maintaining her living quarters in almost cloister-like simplicity.

I thought of Tony's apartment, barren of personality. He had plenty of depth. He merely chose not to express it in his home.

I was the opposite. My tearoom was most definitely expressive. It was meant to be; I had put a lot of effort into making it a beautiful, comfortable haven. My private quarters were less elaborate, but no one could accuse me of austerity.

Realizing my thoughts had wandered, I set the book aside. My teapot was empty, and dusk had fallen outside. A deep blue glow flooded the view through my window. I stood, stretched, and put on the kettle, then stepped out into the hall just in time to see Kris donning her long, black coat.

"Corporate report's on your desk," she said. "Just sign it and stick it in the envelope. No hurry."

"Thanks," I said. "See you tomorrow. Have a good night."

She quirked an eyebrow at me, then headed downstairs. I listened to her receding steps. No other sounds arose from below; Julio and Hanh would have left by mid-afternoon.

I turned on the hall chandelier and strolled over to gaze at O'Keeffe's *White Shell with Red*, hanging outside my suite. The subject was deceptively simple, but the curving lines and gently shaded colors of the shell were mesmerizing, drawing the eye inward, away from the brilliant red background. I knew the image so well I could have closed my eyes and continued to roam it.

The next print over, *Black Cross New Mexico*, was a complete contrast. This was perhaps my least favorite of the group. The cross was not just dominant, it overwhelmed the painting, extending beyond its edges, an in-your-face image from decades before that had become a popular style. I wondered why my mother had bought it, rather than one of O'Keeffe's many lovely flower paintings, of which there were none in this group.

Perhaps I'd add a flower or two. The posters—or rather, reproductions of them—were still available. I went into my office and fired up a browser, setting aside the paperwork Kris had left for me. Yes, the O'Keeffe Museum had lots of posters for sale. I rather liked *Hollyhock Pink with Pedernal*, which appeared to be the closest to a "flower" painting that had been used for the Chamber Music posters. I could add that, but I'd want to find another poster I liked to balance it.

Not right now, though. Whatever splurging I would do this month would be on the trip. I surfed to the Ghost Ranch website to escape the temptation to buy posters, and looked at pictures of lodging instead.

Nat was right, it looked a little rustic. I checked the Abiquiu Inn's site, took one look at the prices, and immediately returned to the Ghost Ranch site. Modest was OK.

Across the hall, my phone rang. I scurried to my suite and caught it on the second ring.

"Hi, Tony!"

"Hey, babe. You eat dinner yet?"

"No, I've been reading."

"Want to go out?"

"Sure!"

"Be right over."

The kettle began to sing. No need for a pot, but I decided to make a quick mug of something to take off the chill. Ginger tea sounded good. While it steeped, I closed the curtains and changed into a plush velour top and warm slacks. I was halfway through the tea when I heard Tony's motorcycle out back.

I met him at the back door. Without discussion he got into my car. I wasn't fond of riding on the back of his bike under the best conditions, and winter nights were definitely out.

"Where to?" I asked as I slid into the driver's seat.

"Del Charro?"

"OK." I started the engine, cranked up the heater, and headed south. Del Charro wasn't trendy, but it was a favorite with the locals and was close enough to the Plaza that it was almost always busy.

"That guy isn't still playing there, is he?" Tony asked.

"That guy you arrested? I don't know. Didn't he go to jail?"

The guy in question was married to a woman who had murdered her sister (my high school classmate) in December. Her charming, musical husband had been sleeping with said sister. A couple of other classmates had also become casualties as the murderer tried to contain the mess she'd made. Tony and I had heard the roving husband playing oldies at Del Charro before his role in the drama—a passive one, but he'd known his wife was guilty—had become evident.

"Not yet," Tony said. "These things take time. And I didn't actually arrest him; we have interceptors for that."

I turned a corner, keeping an eye out for clueless out-of-towner pedestrians. "What's an interceptor?"

"A guy bigger and stronger than me, who can take down a

silverback gorilla if he has to."

"Oh. Armed to the teeth, I take it?"

"And then some."

"Hm."

I found a parking place fairly close to Del Charro, and we walked there at a brisk pace in the chilly night. There was no sign of the philandering husband, or of any musician, when we entered the bar. Canned music was playing. We sat at a table in the back where Tony could command a view of the door, and ordered burgers and beer.

"How's work?" I asked.

"Not bad. Still cleaning up after the holidays."

"Do you get MLK day off?"

"Officially."

"But you might work?"

He shrugged. "Got something better in mind?"

"Well, maybe. I've been thinking of taking a little trip. Just a couple of nights, kind of a stay-cation. I could use a break, and this month is slow."

"Where to?"

"I was thinking, Ghost Ranch?" I said, still unsure about the idea.

The waiter brought our beers at that moment. Tony took a swig of his. I watched, waiting for his reaction to my suggestion.

"Rio Arriba," he said, and took another pull before setting down his pint. "OK."

"OK," I repeated, half surprised, still working on the non-sequitur. Rio Arriba County must be what he meant. Was Abiquiu in Rio Arriba?

"Not much to do up there," Tony added.

"Actually, there is," I said. "I looked up their website. There are lots of activities, talks, concerts, a couple of museums, hiking trails. I'm sort of interested in the Georgia O'Keeffe landscapes tour."

"'Cause of your mom's pictures?"

"Well, yeah."

I was also interested in the tour of O'Keeffe's home and studio in Abiquiu. There was a combination tour that included both that and the landscapes, but I thought five hours might be a bit much for Tony.

"Is it a hike?" he asked.

"No, a bus ride. Or there's a trail ride version."

Tony's face lit with interest. "Horseback?"

I nodded, my mouth full of beer.

"That beats a bus."

"It costs more."

"That's OK. You can ride a horse?"

"Yes."

I hadn't been on horseback since I was a kid, but I figured the ride would be designed for tourists, and therefore minimally exciting. Bored horses, plodding along a well-worn trail, only perking up when the string turned back toward the barn.

"Where'd you learn?" Tony asked.

"Summer camp. You?"

"My uncle had a ranch. I used to help him out over summer vacation. My first paying job."

"Really? Punching cattle?"

"Riding fence, mostly. I helped with the cattle some, but it wasn't that fun."

I sipped my beer, picturing Tony as a vaquero. "Does your uncle still have the ranch?"

"Nah, he sold out and retired."

I had the feeling I shouldn't pursue the subject. Tony's family had some bad memories associated with selling property.

"So, horseback tour," I said. "I'll reserve the tickets, and book us a room at Ghost Ranch. Should we stay three nights? Friday-Saturday-Sunday?"

"Sure."

Wow. This was starting to sound like an actual vacation.

"I'm interested in touring Georgia O'Keeffe's house and studio in Abiquiu, too," I added. "Would you like to join me?"

His eyebrow twitched, then he deliberately smiled. "Make you a deal. I'll go on that tour with you if you'll go on a hike with me."

"Deal. The studio tour will be my treat. I hope you won't be bored."

"Not possible. I'll be with you."

My heart gave a flutter of delight. Tony was not prone to verbal gallantry. He watched me with amusement as he took another swig of beer.

Our burgers arrived, mine loaded with mushrooms and bleu

cheese, Tony's with bacon and green chile. We chatted as we ate, sketching out the details of the trip. We had never spent so much time together, away from work, as we would on this trip. The more we envisioned it, the more I looked forward to it.

By the time we finished our meal, we had the whole trip roughed out: quick dinner in town when we both got off work on Friday night, then drive up to Ghost Ranch and check in. Hike Saturday morning, followed by studio tour. Saturday night there was a concert—a musician from Taos Pueblo who looked interesting. Landscape trail ride on Sunday, maybe another hike, fancy dinner at the Abiquiu Inn Sunday night, then drive home after breakfast on Monday, leaving the rest of that day for doing laundry and whatever else. I drove us back to the tearoom, feeling a buzz of excitement.

"Want to come up?" I asked Tony as we got out of the car.

He gave me a skeptical look. "Not to stay. You're open tomorrow."

"Yes. Want to come up?"

He grinned.

I WAS NOW OFFICIALLY IMPATIENT FOR THE HOLIDAY WEEKEND, but there was one obligation (besides work) that I had to discharge beforehand. I had promised Tony's sister, Angela, a tête-à-tête tea before her college classes resumed. Therefore, the Wednesday before the holiday, I welcomed her into the Violet alcove, my favorite spot in the tearoom for a cozy tea with a friend.

I offered to relieve her of her coat and hang it out in the hall, but she shook her head. "I'd rather keep it, if you don't mind," she said, draping it over her knees as she sat in one of the two violet wing chairs. "I got cold, walking from where I parked," Angela added.

"Not at all," I said, and stepped to the fireplace to add a log. I could hear the party next door, in Dahlia, settling in for their tea.

Angela was a few years younger than Tony, earnestly working to finish her degree in nursing so she could get a job and help support her grandmother. I liked her a lot, and looked forward to spending an hour or so getting to know her better. She had dressed up for tea, in a charming black long-sleeved dress covered with tiny yellow daisies and a little black cocktail hat with a wisp of veil.

"I *adore* that hat!" I said as returned to my chair. Between us stood a low table where the teapot already waited under a cozy. I picked it up and poured for Angela.

"It's Abuela's," she said, rosy with pleasure. "She used to be an amazing clothes horse."

"Oh, really? I'd love to see some photos, if you have them."

"Mama's got a couple of old albums. I'll dig them out before Sunday dinner. You're coming, right?"

"Right."

Sunday dinner was a ritual in the Aragón family. One attended or risked matriarchal disapproval, a rule to which I, as Tony's fiancée, was now subject. A miss required an unquestionable excuse, such as dealing with dead bodies, or being invited to dine at the Governor's mansion.

Rosa brought in our tea tray, and presented it with a glance at Angela and a knowing smile. I had followed Julio's advice and taken Rosa into my confidence about the engagement. Sure enough, Rosa had spared me the task of telling the rest of the staff. She knew Angela was Tony's sister.

Over steaming cups of Margaret's Hope, Angela and I chatted our way through the full, three-tiered tray of afternoon tea savories, scones, and sweets. At first we talked about light things: the holidays, Angela's upcoming classes, the weather. Then, as happens when a conversation goes on long enough, our subjects got deeper. By the time we reached the sweets, I felt brave enough to ask the question I'd been holding.

"Angela, do you think your father would have approved of Tony's and my engagement?"

It was a calculated question, which was a little unfair to Angela. I hoped to read in her response whether she herself approved, because I knew she was too polite to tell me if she didn't.

She gazed at the fire, thinking. "I'm not sure. It was always hard to predict how he'd react. You'd think for sure he'd feel one way, and then it would turn out the opposite." She sipped her tea. "You know, I was only nine when he died, so..."

"I'm sorry. That was thoughtless of me."

"No, no. I don't mind." She set down her cup and took a pear and brie sandwich—one of Julio's inspirations—from the tray. "He never thought much of Tony's girlfriends, but I think he would like you. You're not like any of the others."

I bit my tongue. That could mean a lot of different things. Were Tony's other girlfriends all Hispanic? Were they sexy cheerleader types? Or was it just that they came from his high school, not mine?

"You think about things, and you make Tony think," Angela

added. "Before he met you, he was Mr. Act-First-Think-Later."

"Really? I doubt I was the cause of such a change."

"I think you were. And Mama agrees. She said so, to me."

I swallowed. "Oh?"

"That time we all came to tea, last fall? When we got home, she told me you were the first woman she'd met who might be able to wake Tony up."

"Wake him up?"

Angela nodded. "That's what she said. And then she turned around and told him he better not be rude to you."

"Wake him up from what?" I asked meekly.

She gave me a mischievous glance. "From being full of himself, I think."

I sipped my tea as I thought about that. My early ideas of Tony had certainly included the opinion that he was full of himself. Now I couldn't quite remember when that had changed.

Maybe it hadn't. Maybe I'd just gotten used to it.

But, no. Tony *had* changed. He'd been pretty insufferable at first, and I had not lowered my standards of courtesy in any way that I was aware of.

"He looks up to you," Angela said. "All his other dates, at least the ones I met, he just wanted to get what he could from them, you know? He didn't care what they thought. But he does care, with you."

Now I felt myself blushing. Not knowing what to say, I filled my mouth with a mini cream puff.

"Eh, I'm not telling you anything you don't know," Angela added, proffering her empty cup. I hastened to fill it, and topped up my own, then washed down the cream puff with a sip.

"Angela, would you like to be my bridesmaid?"

She looked up at me, sudden color blooming in her cheeks. "I'd love to!"

"My best friend Gina will be maid of honor," I added, "but I'd like to have you, too."

"Thank you! Yes, I'm honored."

"You can help keep me from being a Bridezilla."

She laughed. "You're about as far from Bridezilla as you can get."

"Well, I'd like to keep it that way."

We finished our teatime on a lighter note, discussing my

bridal colors (should I avoid wisteria?) and where the wedding might be held (I was still uninspired). When the last crumb was consumed and the teapot was empty, Angela rose and slipped her coat on.

"I better get home. Mama's expecting me. Thank you so much!"

"Thank *you*. I'll be wanting to get together with you and Gina to talk about plans—maybe in March?"

"Spring break?"

"Let's compare calendars."

"OK."

I saw her out, slipping past the entrance to Dahlia as unobtrusively as I could on our way to the gift shop. Angela insisted on buying some scones to take home to *Abuela*.

"She's addicted," she told me.

I tucked a couple of cream puffs in with the scones while Rosa rang up the sale, then I handed Angela the box. "My love to your family."

"You'll see them on Sunday."

I smiled and walked with her to the front door, where I gave her a hug. "We'll do this again."

"Yes." She kissed my cheek. "Bye, *manita!*"

I watched her walk to the gate, wondering what she'd called me. I'd have to look it up.

As I returned to the gift shop to make sure Rosa wasn't overwhelmed, I saw the Bird Woman emerging from Dahlia, wearing a far-too-filmy-for-January dress of purple and chartreuse georgette, with a plumed hat worthy of a dowager duchess. Her two guests, middle-aged women, were less splendidly dressed, though they both looked nice enough. Since I didn't recognize them, I assumed this was their first visit to the tearoom. They goggled at me while the Bird Woman broke into a grin.

"Congratulations, sweetie!" she crowed. "I couldn't help overhearing! When's the wedding?"

I winced a little. "In the fall."

"You're gonna be a *beautiful* bride!" she said in a voice that I was sure had carried to the recesses of the main parlor across the hall, if not back to the kitchen.

"That's kind of you, thank you," I answered quietly. "I hope you enjoyed your tea." I followed this with a smile at her guests, which set them tittering.

"Shush!" the Bird Woman told them. "Now hurry up, or we're gonna be late for the movie."

"Happy New Year, Mrs. Olavssen," I called after them, fighting an amused smile.

If I knew anything about her, she'd do Rosa one better and make sure anyone who ever set foot in the tearoom—and possibly the entire population of Santa Fe—knew about my engagement. She still got on my nerves a *little*, but I had learned how truly kind she was, and I was coming to the conclusion that I wanted to be rather like the Bird Woman when I was older.

Heading for the stairs, I spotted a stack of three boxes tucked out of the way beneath the first flight. Looking at the label of the topmost, I confirmed my suspicion: goods for the gift shop. The Valentine's Day merchandise was starting to arrive. I tested the top box's weight, found it not too heavy, and started upstairs with it.

I really should put in a dumb waiter, but even if it was disguised with clever cabinetry, I feared it would mar the architectural beauty of the house. And I might have trouble getting permission for such a change. This was a designated historic building, and there were restrictions. Not to mention that it might be expensive. I hadn't even dared to look into the potential cost.

The box got heavier during the last few steps. Was gravity stronger at higher elevations? Reaching the top of the stairs, I sighed with relief and carried the box into Kris's office. She was away from her desk. I set the box on her credenza and went to the little storeroom tucked behind her desk, where the roof restricted headroom. Turning on the light, I saw that there were already several other boxes in there, and felt a small surge of dismay.

I needed to get in here and find whatever it was Captain Dusenberry had hidden. In December the storeroom had been packed with boxes. By New Year's it had mostly been emptied; now it was starting to fill up again.

I'd come back tonight, after closing. I didn't want to crawl around in there in my nice dress, and I didn't want to disturb Kris.

"Ellen?"

I stepped to the door and turned out the light. Kris was at the tea station that stood in a little nook between our offices, facing the shared doorway that served both rooms.

"Want some tea?" she asked. "I was thinking about making another pot."

"No, thanks, I'm floating," I said. "You go ahead."

She nodded, opening the drawer and setting up the samovar's matching teapot for brewing. Lapsang Souchong, I noted. *Definitely* too much after my tea with Angela.

I stepped past Kris and went into my office, going to my desk. A short stack of lavender message slips awaited me; I glanced through them, dealt with a couple, decided the rest could wait, and brought up my email, still thinking about what might be hidden in the storage room.

Captain Dusenberry, the tearoom's resident ghost, had been killed by two shots fired from a Colt Navy pistol, in his study—the room immediately beneath Kris's office—which was now the tearoom's dining parlor. I wanted very much to know who had fired those shots, and so, I believed, did Captain Dusenberry. The holidays had kept me too busy to pursue the subject, but now I could take it up again.

One possibility was that the captain's killer was a member of the Hidalgo family. I suspected this because I believed Captain Dusenberry had wanted to marry Maria Hidalgo, and that her family had disapproved.

Scrolling back through my emails from December, I hunted for a message that had come in from Sonja at the State Archives during the hectic final week before Christmas. I hadn't had time to do more than glance at it then. There was a lot of other email, so I ended up running a search by sender. This produced the email from Sonja, along with a couple of earlier ones from her that I hadn't finished reading. Ay, yi, yi! I really needed to get more organized about this. Better make a list, but first I read the most recent message.

Ellen -

There's a ton of information about Hidalgo Plaza, so please narrow down your request. I'm attaching a map from 1877, the earliest in our records, but the plaza is much older than that, of course.

You asked earlier about Maria Imelda Fuentes y Hidalgo's papers. We don't have any of them, but I did find an inventory of her personal effects made when she died, along with her obituary. Attaching those for your review.

Have a Merry Christmas!

- Sonja

I saved the attachments to the folder where I was keeping notes and information about the captain's murder. There were other items from Sonja in there that I hadn't yet reviewed. Yes, definitely needed to get organized.

The Hidalgo family had been prominent in Santa Fe for centuries, and still was. Hidalgo Plaza was part of the historic block of buildings on Palace Avenue, across from the Cathedral Basilica of St. Francis. Originally a hacienda belonging to the family, Hidalgo Plaza's historic buildings were now occupied by shops, a bistro, and a fancy restaurant, but the family still managed the property, and might still own it. I had met one of the Hidalgos a couple of months ago, a charming older gentleman named Eduardo who occupied a tiny office just inside the plaza's southwest entrance. He had very kindly allowed me to look at the diaries of Maria Hidalgo, "Tia Maria" as he called her, and to take a picture of an old photo of her that was hanging in his office. Wanting to refresh my memory, I opened that photo and zoomed in.

Maria looked regal, serene, and a little sad, but that might just have been because of how photos were taken back then. Rarely did the subject of such a portrait smile; presumably, the process was considered serious business,. Maria wasn't a beauty, but she was a handsome woman. Her white dress was elegant and austere, ornamented only by a light-colored chain with a watch or a locket, hanging from a pin. Curious which it was, I opened the inventory that Sonja had sent. It listed dresses (each described in brief detail—they were all white except for one black one, presumably worn at funerals); silk lace mantillas (one black, two white); twenty-seven books (no details); a long list of furniture including a bed, desk and chair, and a maple spinet; an ivory chess set; a silver hairbrush, mirror, and shoehorn; hair ornaments (mostly tortoise-shell); a silver ring, and a gold locket with chain.

Aha! So it was a locket, not a watch. I wondered where it was now.

Kris came in with some papers for me to sign. Glancing at the time, I saw that it was almost five, her usual time for leaving. The tearoom would be open until six, then I'd be able to change into grubbies and grub around in the storage room. I signed the papers and handed them back.

"I'm off," Kris said. "See you tomorrow."

"Have a good evening," I told her.

A brief smile flicked across her lips and she turned away. I returned to the email from Sonja and opened Maria's obituary.

It was bland, full of family names, all dust now. About Maria herself, it said, "known for her kindness to all, her charity, and her devotion to good works." Knowing what I knew, I silently added that she was fiercely loyal, and had known only one true love, for whom she had quietly mourned to the end of her days.

I wrote a quick answer to Sonja, requesting any papers on Hidalgo Plaza that referred to Maria, and any information the Archives might have about a concert held in the Santa Fe Plaza on April 7, 1855. That was the Saturday following Captain Dusenberry's death, and I suspected it was the day referred to in the one letter of his to Maria that I had found. This letter had been hidden behind a picture of the Virgin of Guadalupe in the back of Maria's earliest diary, and I had snuck a photo of it during my perusal of the diary. The letter informed Maria that the captain's offer for her hand had been rejected by her father, and that on the occasion of the concert, "A carriage will be waiting nearby to carry us to the church."

Hmm. When Willow Lane and I had discussed this, we'd agreed that he probably meant a Protestant church, which I assumed was the one just across the street from the tearoom. It was currently the First Presbyterian Church of Santa Fe.

I opened a browser and searched for its history, and found out that First Presbyterian hadn't been organized until 1866, eleven years after the captain had died. The Presbyterians had bought "the ruins of a Baptist church that had failed" on land that was now within the intersection of Grant Avenue and Griffin Street.

Yes, that was the one near me; Griffin merged into Grant, forming a "Y" around the grounds of the church, just a little north of the tearoom. I could see the current church from my front window. Apparently the earlier Baptist church had been the only Protestant church in Santa Fe when the Captain had lived here.

I paused, gazing at the sloping ceiling of my office. At that time, this house had been officer's quarters at Fort Marcy Post, and had been assigned to Captain Dusenberry. The army post was large; covering most of my neighborhood from Grant Avenue (which was not yet Grant Avenue) to Lincoln Avenue (ditto), up to the Palace of the Governors, which had been part of the military post in 1855.

How different everything was, now. My house was the only remaining officer's house from Fort Marcy Post. The others had all been torn down and replaced with commercial buildings. Across the street to the west, the historic buildings that remained had been the homes of early merchants and prosperous families— white families, mostly—dating from around the time of Mexican independence in 1821. Once upon a time, my ancestors had lived in that area, but their home was long gone.

If Captain Dusenberry had intended to elope with Maria from the concert and be married in the Baptist church, why had he needed a carriage? It was an easy walk from the Plaza to here. Just a couple of blocks. They could have slipped away during the music, and made their way to the church in just a few minutes.

Unless he wanted the carriage to also take them *away* from the church. Because an elopement to his house might not have been the most comfortable agenda. Angry Hidalgos would have known just where to look.

A quiet tapping made me look toward the doorway. Dee Gallagher, one of my servers, stood there, dark winter coat incongruous over her lavender server's dress.

"Sorry to interrupt," she said. "I just wanted to let you know I'm leaving. We're locked up downstairs."

"OK, thanks," I said.

"And I wanted to ask if it's all right for me to take the afternoon off, on the fifteenth."

"Let me check."

I brought up the staff schedule. The fifteenth was the Friday before a long weekend, the next Monday being a holiday. Dee was already off on the 16th. I could ask Dale or Iz to cover for her on Friday.

"I think so," I said. "I'll let you know tomorrow, all right?"

"Sure. Thanks."

"Planning a vacation?"

"A little one, yeah. Going skiing." Her cheeks dimpled charmingly as she pulled a watch cap over her blonde hair. "Night, Ellen."

"Good night."

Glancing toward the window, I realized it was dark. I should knock off, have some dinner, and then do my searching in the storage room. I looked back at the scatter of open documents on my computer screen. Where was I?

Captain Dusenberry planning to elope with Maria Hidalgo. There were a lot of questions I needed to look into, and several files from Sonja to review. I *still* hadn't opened any of the files she'd sent me with her next-to-last email. She had found those in a search for "Colt Navy Pistol" and "Hidalgo."

Looking up that message, I knew I wasn't up for reading Manuel Hidalgo's diary. Also not hot for reading a collection of letters belonging to a third party. I opened the sales register from Seligman's Mercantile, figuring that wouldn't take too long.

It was a single page from a ledger, listing items sold on March 29, 1855.

That was interesting. Exactly a week before Captain Dusenberry's murder.

Even more interesting: the captain's name was on the list. On that date he had purchased a gold locket and chain.

Oh, my. Could it be that he had bought it as a gift for Maria?

A tingle shot down my arms. I went back to the top of the list and read slowly through it. Most of the purchases were ordinary: cooking staples, tools, candles and lamp oil, and so on. The captain's purchase stood out, as did a half-dozen entries listed as sold to one Tyrone Lea: a "fine gold watch," two boxes of cigars and a humidor, a silk waistcoat, a beaver hat, a pair of Italian shoes, and bottle of French brandy. Mr. Lea was moving up in the world, it appeared.

The second-to-last item on the list was the sale of a Colt Navy Pistol to Reynaldo Hidalgo.

I drew a breath. So Reynaldo had owned a Colt! This could be it!

The last item sold was a pound of sugar, to "R. Smith." One blank line was followed by a tally of purchases made by Seligman's on that date. Three of these were also listed under the name Tyrone Lea: each for twenty boxes of rifle cartridges. So that was how he had afforded all the luxuries. Interesting.

I opened a new document and started a list of tasks, beginning with asking Eduardo Hidalgo if he knew anything about Reynaldo's Colt. If I was very, very lucky, the family would still have it. I added a note to ask if he had a photo of Reynaldo as well. I wanted to know what that man had looked like.

Filling out the list with the other documents from Sonja, I then closed all the files and shut down my computer. After sitting at my desk for so long, it felt good to stand up. I left the office, turned off the light, and headed for my suite.

Still full of afternoon tea, I decided on tomato soup and a salad for dinner. While the soup was heating I changed out of my pretty tea dress and into jeans and a long-sleeved shirt. Perhaps in anticipation of a claustrophobic evening in the storage room, I decided to have my dinner in the sitting area by the front window. I put soup, salad, a glass of white wine and a tumbler of water onto a tray and carried it out into the hall. The floor creaked gently as I walked to the sitting area. I set the tray on the low table and stepped to the window.

Cold radiated from the glass as I gazed down and to the right at the part of the Presbyterian church that was visible. How different things would have been if the captain had survived and married there.

Pulling the drapes closed against the cold, I made myself comfortable on the sofa. Hanging on the wall near the window was the poster of *Blue Green Music*. Though it was abstract, that painting had always made me think of water. It had motion and fluidity, and the colors were soothing and gentle. Well, except for the black bar that rose up out of the bottom center and angled off toward the upper left. Its edges were the sharpest thing in the image.

Contrast. O'Keeffe had been a master of it.

The soup and salad were the perfect counterpart to the rich tea food I'd shared with Angela. Even though January's afternoon tea menu had been designed purposely to be lighter, it was still a filling meal, with scones and three sweets. The salad, especially, was welcome after that indulgence.

Finished, I took my tray back to my suite and washed up, then braided back my hair to keep it out of the way, and headed for Kris's office. The box I had carried up was gone from the credenza; I found it inside the storage room. Turning on both the standing lamp and the bulb that hung from the ceiling, I went to the northwest corner and got down on my hands and knees, peering at the floor.

I had already spent a lot of time knocking on the walls in here, especially the outside walls, with no result. Gut instinct told me the floor was the place to look. Captain Dusenberry had hidden Maria's letters under the floor downstairs; it made sense he'd do the same up here, if he had more to hide.

Which, essentially, he'd told me he had.

I swallowed, remembering Kris's séance, which had taken place in the dining parlor below. Still not comfortable with that event, I focused instead on searching for a loose board.

Unlike the oak floor downstairs, the boards here were wide, rough-cut planks of pine, probably unfinished to begin with, but some time in the past hundred and more years someone had decided to varnish them. They were now darkened with time and a good deal of engrained dust. I poked and pressed at the end of each board, but found none that were loose. Working my way from east to west along the north wall, I eventually encountered the boxes. I carried them out into Kris's office, determined to examine every inch of the storage room floor.

I did. No loose boards.

Frustrated, I sat back on my heels and gazed back toward the west wall. A thin, dark line near the west wall caught my attention. I crawled over to it, and found that it was the end of a board that was a tiny fraction of an inch—maybe a millimeter—higher than its neighbor. I poked at it. Felt solid, didn't budge. Still, it was the only difference I'd found.

I got to my feet, taking care not to whack my head against the low side of the sloping ceiling, and went across the hall to my suite. I had a toolbox under the sink in the kitchenette, from which I extracted a hammer and a small crowbar. Thus armed, I returned to the storeroom to attack the uneven board. The end that was higher was perhaps two feet from the wall.

Time was my friend in this case. It had shrunk the pine boards over the decades, so they were no longer snugged tight together. I was able to work one end of the crowbar between the high board and its neighbor. With a few taps from the hammer, I got the bar beneath the lower edge of the board. Gently, I pressed it back, working to lift the end of the board. It took some wiggling, and moving the bar back and forth a couple of times, but eventually I got the end of the board up about a half inch above its neighbor.

Pausing, I set the bar beneath the board to keep it up, and went to my suite for a flashlight. When I aimed it into the gap beneath the board, I let out a sigh.

Nothing under there but dust. I shone the light into all the corners I could see, but the struts supporting the floor ran crosswise to the boards, so the space I'd uncovered was only about a foot long. It was empty.

If I pulled the board out, I might see more. I might also not be able to get it back in.

Was I nuts? Tearing up the floor in my house? If I found nothing under this board, how many more would I be willing to pull up?

Movement caught my eye. I sat back and looked at the board. Its shadow was shifting back and forth.

I looked up, blinking at the light of the bare bulb hanging above. It was swaying slightly at the end of its cord.

"All right, all right," I muttered. "Might as well finish it."

I moved the crowbar aside, took hold of the board, and tugged it toward me. It came free with a few small "pops" of cracking varnish.

Two more struts were now visible, one between me and the wall, and one just a handspan from the wall. I put down the board and picked up my flashlight, shining it into the spaces. Nothing between the first and second struts. I scooted closer to the wall and aimed the light into the small gap near the wall.

Almost the same color as the boards, a small pouch of heavy leather lay tucked against the outside wall. It reminded me of the cartridge pouch worn by Mr. Quentin, the reenactor who had talked about Captain Dusenberry during the ghost tour teas we had hosted with Willow in October.

That was another item for my to-do list: talk to Mr. Quentin about a metal detector.

Later.

I reached into the gap and took hold of the leather pouch. It was hard, belt leather: old and dry and dusty. Heavier than I expected. Definitely not empty. I lifted it out carefully.

Yes, it might be a cartridge pouch, or maybe some other belt pouch. Mr. Quentin's had a brass plate with "US" stamped on it; this one was unadorned. There were slots in the back, where a belt could thread through, but there was no belt with it. I held it in my hands, almost unwilling to believe it. Captain Dusenberry had told me to look here, and this is what I had found.

I swallowed, then sneezed. The dust was getting to me. Leaving the tools and my flashlight, I carefully stood and carried the pouch out into Kris's office and through to the hall. There I brushed off the worst of the dust, then took the pouch to the sitting area and put it on the table while I brushed dust off of myself.

Sitting down, I carefully lifted the pouch's front flap. Inside were two soft leather drawstring bags—one full and heavy, one nearly empty—and a folded piece of paper. I set them all on the table, hesitant to open them. I felt a little like an intruder, prying into these things.

But they were mine. They were part of the house, and the house belonged to me.

Deciding I should document them, I fetched my camera and took several pictures of the pouch and its contents. Then I began to examine them.

The paper, which I unfolded carefully, was a marriage certificate that had not been filled in. Blank lines awaited the names and signatures of the bride and groom and their witnesses. Tucked inside it was a receipt: fare for two passengers on a northbound stagecoach.

So he *had* planned to take Maria away from Santa Fe after the wedding. Maybe for a honeymoon? He wouldn't have abandoned his post, so he must have made arrangements for someone to cover his job until he returned.

Add to the list: check the captain's official correspondence.

I opened the smaller pouch, after a little trouble with the strings, which had been wound very tightly around the drawstring opening several times. Inside were two plain gold rings, one smaller than the other.

Wedding bands.

I couldn't help glancing at my engagement ring. I turned the rings this way and that, looking for any engraving on the inside, but they were unmarked.

Finally, I picked up the heavy pouch. In my hand, it was the size of a small apple. When I opened it, I found it was full of coins, mostly silver, but a few gold. Some were tiny, smaller than a dime.

Oh. My. God.

These might be worth a lot. So many coins! Was this the captain's life savings?

Carefully, so as not to drop any, I took a few coins out and spread them on the other pouch with the rings, then took more photographs of everything. My hands were shaking a little.

This was amazing. This was a treasure! Here were all of Captain Dusenberry's hopes and dreams. They had waited hidden beneath the floor for over a century, never to be realized.

Why had he led me to them? My finding them wouldn't change the past. They were proof of his intentions, but what good would that do him now?

Was this his gift to me, simply because I cared?

I sat gazing at everything for a while, feeling rather stunned. Finally I decided I needed to protect these items, put them away someplace safe. They belonged in my safety deposit box, actually. I would take them there tomorrow.

Carefully, I put the coins and the rings back in their bags, and slid the stage tickets back into the folded license. I tucked them all into the pouch, closed it, then carried it into my office and locked it in my desk.

Tomorrow morning, I'd take it to the bank. Better take Maria's letters, too, I decided. This was becoming an important collection of artifacts.

Feeling a little melancholy, I returned to the storage room. For good measure, I turned on the flashlight and peered into the little gap to make sure there was nothing else hidden in there. It was empty now.

The board slid back into place pretty easily, and when I pushed, it settled down level with the rest of the floor. My fiddling with it had apparently loosened the fit just enough that it no longer stood proud.

Well, if I ever needed a place to hide something secret, I had it now.

I moved the boxes back into the storeroom, then turned out the lights and closed the door. I felt drained and exhausted, and now I had even more questions. I put away my tools, then took the camera into my office and turned on my computer so I could download the photos.

The computer time showed 11:49. *Really?* Ay, yi, yi!

I saved a copy of the photos onto a thumb drive, which I locked away with the pouch and Maria's letters. Then I shut down the computer and went across to my suite to shower off the dust.

I DREAMED OF A WEDDING ON THE SANTA FE PLAZA. A small orchestra was playing on the bandstand, and I waltzed with Captain Dusenberry on the grassy grounds. We were both dressed in white, though I wasn't the bride. There was more to the dream, but I didn't remember it after my alarm went off.

The day was crazy busy. The tearoom was nearly sold out; reservations had ramped up that week, possibly in advance of the holiday weekend. I was on the go from 7:00 a.m. on, and only Nat's assistance enabled me to get away long enough to take my treasures to the bank. I dusted off an attaché case that I hadn't used since college for the occasion, using it to protect the leather pouch—which I also wrapped in a clean dishtowel—and the box containing Maria's letters, as well as the thumb-drive of photos.

I had to rent a bigger safety deposit box to contain everything. I winced at the cost, and at the extra time it took, but there was no question about it. These things had to be kept safe. Even more, now, I felt an obligation to consider donating them—or maybe selling them—to the historical museum. They should be appraised, I realized. Claudia Pearson might be able to recommend an appraiser, but it would have to wait. I was leaving town the next evening. On my vacation—the first in over a year.

Returning to the tearoom, I put the empty attaché case in my office and poured myself some tea. I hadn't told anyone about my find, not even Nat. I *would* tell them, but I wasn't ready yet. I was still a bit stunned by it.

Captain Dusenberry's treasures had waited hidden in my floor for a hundred and sixty years. They could wait a few more days.

Friday evening, it was already dark by the time Tony and I left Santa Fe for Ghost Ranch. We'd opted for a quick green chile cheeseburger at Lotaburger on the way out of town, saving our splurge money for the big Sunday night dinner. I sipped what was left of my chocolate malt and nudged the heater up a click as I steered my car into the flood of northbound traffic, a river of red taillights flowing into the darkness. Commuters, mostly, on their way home. Fewer cars were driving into Santa Fe.

"Why is it called Ghost Ranch?" Tony asked.

"I don't know. I thought you would."

He shot me a mischievous look. "You're the native."

"So are you. And you're the cop. Don't you ever have to deal with stuff north of town?"

"Not that far north. That's Rio Arriba County. Not my jurisdiction."

"Oh."

"Anyway, it's an Anglo tourist place," Tony said as he reclined his seat a notch and shifted to get comfortable. "I figured you would have looked it up."

"Sorry to disappoint." I took one long, gurgly pull at the remains of the malt, then put the cup down. I was tempted to respond to the "Anglo tourist" remark, but I didn't want to start this weekend with a disagreement. "I'm sure someone there can tell us. Some ghost story."

"Yeah."

Also, Tony was right. The book Nat had given me had filled in my knowledge. Ghost Ranch had been a dude ranch in the early 20th century, and it *was* primarily patronized by Anglos at that time. Rich Anglos from "back East," specifically. White folks looking for adventure in the "Wild West." Georgia O'Keeffe didn't precisely fall into that class, because she was looking for solitude rather than adventure, but she had stayed at Ghost Ranch, fallen in love with the scenery, and cajoled the ranch's owner into selling her a rather remote old adobe ranch house on the property. She'd spent several years there (when she wasn't in New York), and painted a bunch of paintings of the surrounding landscape. This was the area through which we'd ride on our horseback tour.

Ghost Ranch was now owned by the Presbyterian Church, and operated as a retreat and education center. Still, admittedly, patronized mostly (but not exclusively) by Anglos. Habits of thought and attitude were slow to change. Even though everyone was welcome, New Mexicans tended to think of it as a place for Anglos. A tourist place.

Well, so we were tourists in our home state this weekend. So be it.

Traffic remained heavy until we were past Española, then dwindled to nearly nothing. Now I noticed the moon—full, or nearly so—riding over the Sangre de Cristos to the east. Being busy driving, I hadn't noticed it rising. Our destination was to the northwest, so we were angled away from the mountains a bit, toward some other mountains and bluffs and cliffs. Bathed in moonlight, they were silent and majestic. I remembered the book about O'Keeffe saying she'd climbed onto the roof of her Ghost Ranch house every evening to look at the sky.

Well, New Mexico skies *were* amazing. The brightness of the moon washed away most of the stars, even as it painted the land in light you could read by.

We passed the Abiquiu Inn, brightly light and nestled among tall, leafless cottonwoods that reached skeletal branches toward the moon. Its parking lot was full of cars, mostly SUVs. A large, cubic building that I didn't remember stood to the west of the inn; the new Georgia O'Keeffe welcome center. Abiquiu proper— including O'Keeffe's second home and studio—was on the left, up a hill, a short distance farther along the highway. The road that led to it began opposite a large convenience store: Bode's. After that, a whole lot of empty scenery for a while.

We drove past Abiquiu Lake, but didn't get much of a look at it. Much lower than the road, and frequently obscured by mesas or hills.

I almost missed the gate to Ghost Ranch on the north side of the road. It wasn't lit, but it was tall, and the cow's skull logo caught my eye just in time to slow me down for the turn. A cattle crossing sign just inside the gate had been augmented with a tiny, cartoon UFO, which gave me a chuckle. The road was unpaved, and the smell of New Mexico dust began to seep through the heater into the car. I drove slowly, wary of potholes, but the road was actually broad and even, well-maintained. It rose steadily; we were driving into the hills.

A light shone out ahead, from a building up on top of a hillside to the left. I stopped in a broad, graveled parking lot that fronted the hill, looking up toward a long, low building reminiscent of a ranch house. We got out and climbed a number of irregular steps to where the comforting porch light welcomed us outside a set of double doors.

The place seemed deserted. We stepped inside and looked around at bulletin boards, two closed office doors, a closed "Trading Post" gift shop, a closed snack bar. Straight ahead there were restrooms, which I was grateful to see, and just to the left inside the front door a brightly lit room with a reception counter. I poked my head in.

"Evening!" a blonde woman about my age said, looking up from a book. She was white as could be and looked nothing like a ranch hand—Protestant, probably, since that church owned Ghost Ranch. She wore jeans and a pretty sweater with geometric patterns in cream, gold, and blue. Also a name badge that I couldn't read this far away. She got up and came forward to the counter, smiling. "Rosings?"

"Yes," I said.

"Come on in, I'll get you checked in." she said, typing on a computer keyboard. "You're the last ones tonight. Glad you made it."

Financial details were exchanged. I noted the name badge bore the Ghost Ranch cow skull logo and said "Debbie, Guest Services Specialist." Something about her demeanor convinced me that Debbie was probably a Presbyterian. Along with the keycode to our room, she gave us a map of the grounds, including a confusing number of buildings and the starting points for several hiking trails.

"You're in the Ghost House," she said, drawing on the map with a highlighter. "It's just up the road right here. There's a parking space for you right nearby."

"The Ghost House?"

"That's right. Oldest building on the ranch. There are some photos and displays on the public side of it—that's open all the time, but don't worry, nobody'll bother you. And it's on the walking tour at 11:30 in the morning. That's free to guests, so be sure to catch it."

I had opted to pay more for a room with a private bathroom, preferring not to share bathrooms in the more dorm-like lodgings. When I'd called to make reservations, the person I talked to had said I'd reserved the last available room with a private bath that weekend. They had *not* informed me of its name.

The Ghost House. My luck.

"Are there any…actual ghosts, in the Ghost House?" I asked.

The woman smiled. "Depends who you talk to. Legends, sure. It was built by the Archuleta brothers, the first people to live here. Colorful legends—you'll hear all about them on the tour."

"Legends, but no hauntings?" Tony asked.

She blinked at him. "Well, some folks say they hear voices outside the house at night. But I've never heard them." She looked at me. "Don't worry, nothing dramatic's ever been reported."

"Oh," I said. "Good."

Tony gave me an amused glance. "Think the Captain'll be jealous?"

I shot him a repressive look, and tucked the map into my pocket.

We returned to the car for a drive that was extremely short indeed. In fact, we might as well have walked, but it was better to park close to our room, which turned out to be on the north end of the Ghost House. The south end was lit by a bright porch light illuminating a charming courtyard inside an adobe wall. A hand-carved wooden sign on the *portal* labeled it "GHOST HOUSE" in spooky lettering, and another sign nearby announced, "ALWAYS OPEN."

This gave me dubious feelings about our privacy. However, the door to our room was around the other end of the building, unassuming and easy to overlook. It was guarded by two gigantic cottonwoods, and marked with another hand-carved sign that said "STEP DOWN" (no handicapped access, apparently). The imposing keypad lock was the only comparatively modern-looking thing about the place. Tony punched in the code, and we carried our bags inside, dutifully stepping down the four inches from the threshold to the floor.

We found ourselves in a small bedroom with a double bed, on which two sets of towels had been left. Adjacent was a tiny bathroom. A wooden dresser stood against the wall opposite the bed. I opened a second door to the left, hoping for a closet, and instead finding another room, similar-sized, containing nine mismatched straight-backed chairs and no table. The chairs were obviously stashed here for storage purposes, although they were arranged in a circle around the room and could have been used for a small meeting. This room had two windows overlooking the walled courtyard to the south and the road to the east, and a small kiva fireplace in one corner, its opening blocked by a particle board insert. No fires allowed, probably at the insistence of some insurance company. Both rooms featured fairly simple and rather dated Southwestern décor, and were haunted by that familiar dusty smell that inhabits old buildings. A polite note on the dresser reminded us that there was no maid service.

A bit rustic, yes.

There was an ancient tube television in the room with the chairs, which surprised me, as the website had indicated there were no televisions. A small sign taped to the bottom of the box stated that DVDs were available from the library, and I saw that the TV had a built-in player. Curious, I switched it on, and was rewarded with a screen full of snow.

"You want the top two drawers or the bottom two?" Tony called from the bedroom.

"Top, please."

I went back there to stow my clothes in the dresser. I had brought a nice dress for our fancy dinner on Sunday. I found a hook on the back of the bathroom door and hung it there. Once I was unpacked, I sat on the bed and lifted the curtain to look out the window, the bottom of which was barely two feet above the level of the ground outside; the building was partially bermed into a hillside. Or maybe the hillside had gradually begun to swallow the old house. Through the window I saw the bases of the two cottonwoods, and just beyond them, a deer, grazing contentedly, bathed in moonlight.

"Tony!" I called, *sotto voce*.

He joined me, and we watched the deer until it ambled away, hidden by the trees. Bright lights marked other buildings to the east, and the moonlight illuminated the road that led to them. I took out my map and identified the Agape Worship Center, the Library, and the Dining Hall, where we'd be served the breakfast that was included with our room, and additional meals for a modest fee.

Perhaps the most interesting thing about this place was the silence.

Santa Fe wasn't a booming city, but it did have traffic noise and whatnot at a low level most of the time. Ghost Ranch, well away from the highway and miles from the nearest village, was absolutely still.

I liked it. The feeling took me back to summer camp, where I'd first encountered the vast quietude of New Mexico's mountains. There'd been a river running past our cabin at camp; I could almost imagine hearing it, though there was no river here.

Tony went into the bathroom. I stretched out on my back on the bed and closed my eyes, listening to the quiet. After a moment, a high-pitched yipping, in multiple voices, commenced in the distance, barely audible. A thrill went down my spine; this was a sound I hadn't heard in years. Coyotes, greeting the moon.

That took me away from summer camp and into the national parks, camping out with Joe and our parents. The coyote calls had sent me crawling into Mom's sleeping bag, shivering at the alien sound.

Tony came out of the bathroom. I opened my eyes and sat up, gesturing for him to be quiet and listen. He did so, while the ancient plumbing settled down. After a minute he smiled slowly.

"Like on *Tio's* ranch," he whispered.

I nodded understanding. Tony sat next to me and slid his arms around my waist, nuzzling my neck. The skirling cries stopped, then after a minute they started up again, farther away, just on the edge of hearing.

Tony started kissing my neck, and I stopped hearing the coyotes.

Light, indirect and muted, disturbed my sleep. Gradually I woke to an unfamiliar space. Smells of not-my-laundry soap and old-building conflicted with the comfortable smell of Tony. I relaxed, enjoying the warmth of his embrace, letting go of the puzzling place until eventually I remembered. We were at Ghost Ranch.

Tony was awake, I realized. He was holding too still to be asleep. I slid my hand under his shoulder, which set him in motion, kissing me hungrily, sliding limbs languorously. He unceremoniously moved me where he wanted me, then made delicious love to me until we were both sated.

I became aware of a bird singing outside, somewhere nearby. Tony's stomach gurgled as if in reply.

"Hungry?" I asked.

"Mm-hm."

I kissed his collar-bone, which happened to be within reach. He kissed my forehead, then rolled out of bed and plodded into the bathroom. I heard the shower turn on.

Sighing contentedly, I stretched, then got up and fetched my robe from the dresser. The air was chilly, making me wish I'd thought to bring slippers as well. I pulled on a pair of socks (I'd brought extras of those), and peeked through the curtains, looking for the bird, but didn't spot it.

I showered while Tony dressed, then we walked up the dusty road to the dining hall for breakfast. The view beyond the (admittedly rustic) buildings was spectacular. To the north, a high mesa ended abruptly, with a pair of stone pillars of white rock, carved by wind and rain, standing just to the left of the main cliff. One pillar was a bit larger than the other. I was certain that every male who saw that pillar had specific thoughts about what it resembled, hopefully private. Tony kept his private, for which I was grateful.

We'd been directed to enter the dining hall by a small door on the north, which turned out to lead to a cafeteria style food line. We turned in our breakfast tickets and helped ourselves to scrambled eggs and toast. There was also oatmeal, cold cereal, and a yogurt bar. The food wasn't fancy but it looked fresh and well-prepared. Emerging into the dining hall proper, Tony and I discovered a long, tall table bearing assorted condiments, where we ladled green chile sauce over our scrambled eggs. We found seats at one of the long dining tables set diagonally across the room, each formed from three or four large rectangular tables. Except for the diagonal placement, this arrangement also rang summer camp bells.

The room was big enough to host a couple hundred people, I thought, though not all of the space was filled, and stacks of chairs and folded tables against the wall at the far end implied a full house was not expected. The dining tables currently set up would seat at least fifty, but there were nowhere near that many in the hall. There might not be that many visitors here in January.

The east end of the hall featured a massive floor-to-ceiling wall of river rock, which totally overshadowed the actually-not-small fireplace set into its center. To the south, the cinder block walls were interrupted at intervals by tall windows that let in a flood of daylight, softening the otherwise industrial look of the hall. Interspersed with the windows were several doors leading out to a large covered *portal*, where picnic tables provided extra seating. Too cold now, but might be nice at lunchtime.

"I didn't see any napkins," Tony said, putting down his plate next to mine. I gestured toward the paper towel racks at intervals along the table.

"Oh," he said. "A bit rustic."

"Yeah."

"Coffee," Tony added, and got up, making a beeline for the drinks counter against the kitchen wall. Racks of mugs and glasses stood beside a variety of machines for dispensing juice, water, and of course, coffee. I waited until he got back, then went over to investigate the array myself.

No tea, no milk. *Very* rustic. But wait—there was cold cereal on the cafeteria line. There had to be milk.

I looked around until I spotted a second, smaller drinks station in between two of the windows on the south wall. This had a coffee machine and a small refrigerator with cartons of milk (including non-dairy milk), half-and-half, and cream. On the other side of a partition were a rack of mugs and a small metal chest of drawers, like a modern apothecary chest, containing a fairly decent selection of teas, albeit in teabags. Conventional black teas, chais, herbals—not bad, but I had brought a small electric kettle and some leaf tea with me, so I could make myself a decent cuppa later on. I would have to borrow a mug from the dining hall, as there were none in our room. Meanwhile, I opted for coffee with a generous dollop of cream.

Tony was tucking into his eggs when I returned. I was hungry, too. I spread jam on my toast, looking around the hall at the other visitors.

There were perhaps two dozen of us, not counting those still in the cafeteria line. Most were Anglos, and most of these looked like out-of-staters. Something about the way they carried themselves, and the way they dressed, just said "not New Mexican."

The handful of Hispanics, on the other hand, were probably locals. Maybe some were employees of the ranch. Some wore casual business attire, others wore jeans and denim or flannel shirts, making them look more like ranch hands.

I noticed two men sitting together—a white guy with curly red hair and a stubbly beard, and a younger, wiry Hispanic guy. Both were dressed in jeans and long-sleeved, western-style shirts. The white guy caught me looking at him and leered back. I glanced away.

A family seated in the next row of tables to ours—mother, father and son about ten or twelve years old—were the only African Americans in the hall. The mother caught my interest; her casual clothes were rather stylish, and she moved with a grace that said "finishing school." Her son was slightly pudgy and glued to his phone. The father was large, equally pudgy, and loud. He wore a leather tour jacket with "Texans" across the back in wide, block letters, with a logo resembling a stylized, red-white-and-blue bull's head. I'd never seen that logo, but then, I didn't follow football. If I hadn't observed them interacting, I would not have paired him with his elegant wife, who shot him a repressive glance as he complained about the lack of televisions in the dining hall. The large cluster of diamonds set in gold flashing on her left hand attested to her husband's prosperity, if not his taste.

Or was I wrong in assuming it was his prosperity, and not hers? I had trouble imagining why an elegant and independently wealthy woman would marry such a man. An elegant woman in need of support, however...

"I give 'em two years, tops," Tony said, mopping up the last of his chile with a piece of toast.

"Oh?" I was surprised by the comment. Tony didn't often voice such opinions.

"He doesn't respect her. Want more coffee?" He stood up, mug in hand.

"No, thanks. I think I'll make some tea back in the room."

"We're hiking, remember."

"I remember."

"When's the studio tour?"

"After lunch. One o'clock. Shall we do the walking tour, if

we're back in time?"

"Mm." He sauntered off toward the coffee urn.

I glanced at my watch. Not yet nine, and I wouldn't mind waiting to hike until it got a bit warmer. I could take or leave the walking tour.

Loud, male voices drew my attention. The black dad was in a quasi-friendly dispute over football with a broad-shouldered white guy in a crisp, green-and-white Western shirt and jeans that looked new. Not caring much about football, I carried my plate and mug to the dishwashers' station and joined Tony.

"I think I'll go back to the room and make that tea."

"I'll come with you," Tony said. "We can look at the trail map and pick out a hike."

He chugged his coffee in three impressive pulls, then took the mug to the washing counter as we passed on our way to the exit. Reminded that I needed a mug, I darted to the coffee bar to snag a clean one. The football dispute was getting louder and less friendly. The nattily-dressed white guy had somehow increased his shoulder breadth and begun to resemble a bull, and his gaze was becoming a glare. The "Texans" fan grinned and kept goading, enjoying the other's irritation. I glanced around, looking for the elegant wife, but didn't see her or the son.

Outside, the only argument was between a couple of jays up in the cottonwoods. I breathed a sigh of relief.

Maybe the Abiquiu Inn would have been worth the extra expense. I hadn't counted on fellow guests making life uncomfortable. Wasn't this the sort of place one visited to get away from things like football?

Back at the Ghost House, Tony got out the hiking map while I made tea. I chose to do this in the Room of Many Chairs, where my kettle and tea things would be out of the way. The only electrical plug was the one into which the old TV was plugged. I unplugged it, skeptical of the integrity of its gently-desiccating cord, and plugged in my travel kettle, which I'd filled from the sink. I chose a chair with a solid wood, mostly-flat seat to serve as my table, on which I arranged all the tea things.

I had brought two kinds of tea: Darjeeling and Assam. I went for the Darjeeling, wanting something lighter after the coffee. I poured a mug, added a bit of sugar, then covered the teapot with a cozy and carried my mug to the bedroom, where I joined Tony on the bed, which was still unmade.

Oh, yes. We'd have to deal with that. An opportunity to create policy for future shared housework.

"This is the trail for Chimney Rock," Tony said, pointing at a dotted line that meandered off westward on the map. "I assume that's the big rock pillar we saw. Might be a bit steep."

"Shall we hike in the other direction?"

"Okay." He peered at the map again. "Interesting name on this one."

He pointed to a trailhead that on the east side of the map, labeled "Matrimonial Mesa."

"Oh," I said. "Well, of course, we must hike there."

Tony glanced up at me with a grin. I leaned back and sipped my tea.

"We could elope," he said blandly.

"Nat would throttle me. She's already designated herself my substitute parent. She's looking forward to making a big fuss."

Tony grimaced slightly.

"And then there's Gina. She's my maid of honor, and if I skip out on her, I'll never hear the end of it."

"It was just a thought," Tony said. "I'm gonna change my shoes."

I fetched myself a second cup of tea, then watched while he put on a pair of battered hiking boots. "Did Angela tell you she's going to be my bridesmaid?" I asked.

"Uh-huh. Thanks for asking her. She's jazzed."

"She called me something...*mieta?*"

"Probably '*manita*'."

"Yes, that was it. What does it mean?"

"It means sister, kind of."

"I thought sister was *hermana*."

"Yeah, *manita* is kind of like sister and best buddy rolled into one."

"Aww!" I felt myself blushing. "I'm honored. I really like Angela."

"She likes you too. You done?"

I finished the last swallow of tea. "Yes. Let me wash up."

"You remember your boots?"

"Yes. Both kinds."

Hiking boots for this morning, boots with a heel for the trail ride. I didn't have actual cowboy boots, but I had some high-rise leather boots with a half-inch heel, which was the important thing. A heel to keep the foot from slipping through the stirrup, and a shoe sturdy enough (one hoped) to protect the foot should a horse's hoof happen to come down on it.

Ah, summer camp memories! I was happy to recall being told that horses actually dislike stepping on humans. (Too squishy.)

When I had tidied and put away my tea things, I put on a pair of thick socks and my hiking boots. Tony, impatient to go, began scrolling through something on his phone. I grabbed a sweater, stuffed my phone, wallet, and keys into the pockets of my jeans; and picked up my water bottle and hat.

"OK," I said, joining Tony by the door.

We stepped out into a beautiful morning. The early chill had faded, and the sky was a brilliant turquoise above sandstone cliffs to the north, and east, and the more distant bluffs to the west. To the south, beyond the highway and Abiquiu Lake, was the mesa called *Cerro Pedernal*, made famous by O'Keeffe's many paintings of it.

Birds chattered and argued in the trees as we headed back toward the dining hall, then struck east across an open field. I put on my hat—a plain, round, brimmed one of black straw—to ward off the bright winter sun. Tony had donned a Capital High Jaguars gimme hat and shades. He pulled the hiking map out of his back pocket, and consulted it to learn where we needed to go to find the right trailhead.

The map showed only the start and end of the Matrimonial Mesa trail, and they were some distance apart. Who knew what might go on between them? The starting point was behind a long, dorm-like building marked "Staff House" on the map. As we headed around one end of it, a man in a western shirt, chaps over jeans, and a cowboy hat came out of one of the doors.

It was the red-headed guy from the dining hall. He grinned. I looked away.

The trail crossed a wide, dry riverbed that made me grateful we were not here in flash-flood season, and climbed up the far bank onto a steep hillside. A makeshift wooden ramp, perhaps twenty feet long and covered with asphalt paper, offered dubious assistance for reaching the top of the hill. Tony went up it like a mountain goat. I climbed more slowly, not trusting the footing on what felt like a forty-five degree incline. I was grateful that my boots had a decent tread, or I'd have been slipping.

Tony reached out a hand as I neared the top, and squeezed my fingers as I joined him. "You good?"

"Yes," I said, adjusting my hat, annoyed that I was slightly out of breath. I climbed up and down stairs a lot during business hours, but that long, steep slope was more than I was used to.

"Good," Tony said.

The trail continued upward at a much more reasonable slope, went over the shoulder of the hill, and twined down the far side. Here, away from the river bed, the landscape was more dry, with mostly piñon and juniper. Anything deciduous looked dead at this season.

Through many more ups and downs, we gradually ascended the mesa. I kept expecting to reach the usual flat-topped bluff crowning cliffs of sandstone or maybe basalt that defined my idea of a mesa. Instead, the trail ran along spines of rock so narrow I had to concentrate on my footing and not give in to the temptation to glance at the surrounding landscape. One wrong step would mean a tumble down a steep, rocky decline.

At the top of one hill the trail diverged, offering a choice of spines to traverse, and a flat space ten feet or so across where we could stand and rest a moment without risk of vertigo. I looked up at the cliffs to the east, much higher yet than where we stood, a medley of reds, oranges, and golds topped with a dark fringe of evergreens. The bluff toward the north that terminated in Chimney Rock was mostly white, probably composed of tuff that had once been volcanic ash rather than the rich, organic mix of sandstone that had once been a sea-floor.

I pointed toward the white mesa. "Makes me think of the White Place."

Tony gave me a look. Though I couldn't see his eyes through his shades, the eyebrows displayed skepticism.

"O'Keeffe's White Place. One of the places she liked to paint. It's more to the east, though, I think. But the rock looks similar."

"Oh. Are we going to go there?"

"We could. It isn't part of Ghost Ranch, but it's not too far. If we have spare time we could drive over."

Unlike the Black Place, which was over a hundred miles to the west and not easily accessible. It might even be on private land.

The biography told of O'Keeffe and a friend driving across country in O'Keeffe's Model-A Ford to camp in solitude at the Black Place. That was decades ago, of course, but I had the impression it was still not reachable by developed roads.

Tony glanced at the white mesa and took a swig from his water bottle. Reminded, I drank from my own. My father's hiking advice from years ago echoed: always hydrate, even if you don't think you need to.

"Which way?" Tony asked, indicating the branching trail.

One branch headed eastish, toward the spectacular cliffs, diving steeply and then ascending again. A couple of ridges over I saw three people hiking that way. I looked along the other branch, which was more level and ran southeast. To the south was *Pedernal*, and a little west of that I saw a glimpse of water—a corner of Abiquiu Lake.

"Let's try this one," I said, preferring the trail that ran more horizontally.

"Yeah. I think that's going to connect us with the other end on the map."

Tony led off along the new spine. I refrained from admiring the view until we paused again.

We had reached the broad, flat mesa top I'd been expecting. The ground spread before us, dotted by trees. A ramada stood perhaps fifty yards away, and a dirt road proceeded beyond it. This was the part of Matrimonial Mesa that was actually big enough to accommodate a wedding.

"OK," Tony said, nodding toward the ramada. "That must be where people get married. And that road probably connects with the entrance road."

I nodded and took a drink of water. "Would have been easier to get here by car," I remarked.

"Yeah, but that's not the point."

"True."

Driving, we would not have walked across heart-pumping spines of rock, and the landscape would have had less impact through the windows of a car. Also, we would not have had any exercise.

"I wonder who got married here first," I mused. "The name must have been because of a wedding."

Tony shrugged. "Or a lot of weddings. But you're right

—'matrimonial' is a fancy Anglo word. I bet it was the original owner of the ranch."

I found myself feeling slightly offended, but let it go. I did have a partiality for fancy Anglo words.

I strolled toward the ramada, curious. There was no information posted there; it was merely a shelter. Merely a suggestion. Sort of like our engagement—though being here, alone together, was making it all feel a little more real.

I toyed with the idea of getting married here. The setting could hardly be more magnificent. I wasn't really interested in a "destination" wedding, but this wasn't Hawaii or Las Vegas, requiring an expensive hotel stay. Our friends and family could come here for the wedding and be home that night, if they wished.

But was this stark place, this dusty mesa top, really where I wanted to exchange vows with Tony?

He stepped into the ramada beside me, slipped his arm around my waist, and surprised me with a kiss.

"Oh!"

He grinned. "Just practicing."

"Well in that case, allow me to assist."

I wrapped my arms around his neck and invited a much more thorough kiss. Tony obliged.

"Better?" he said after a moment.

"Yes. But I think you should keep practicing."

4

THE SOUND OF A CAR INTERRUPTED US, and we stepped apart instinctively, though it turned out the car wasn't visible. Probably on the
entrance road, down below the mesa.

"We could walk back on the road," Tony said.

"Boring. Let's go back the way we came."

"OK."

The sun was warm now, and I tied my superfluous sweater
around my hips before we started back for the narrow trails. I had
drunk more than half my water, so I began rationing it. Cautious
sips. I was starting to get hungry, too. I'd be ready for lunch by
the time we got back.

Tsk. Should've brought some nuts, or gorp, and extra water. I
could imagine my brother Joe frowning in disapproval.

Well it was a short hike, and we knew that. And we weren't
the only ones out here. I dismissed phantom Joe back to New
York, where he belonged.

Oh. I'd have to invite him to the wedding.

I grimaced. His visit at Christmas hadn't been entirely fun.
He'd shown some attitude where Tony was concerned, and while
I'd told him in no uncertain terms what I expected in the way of
courtesy, I knew that old habits, and old attitudes, die hard.

Mom would have smoothed things over. I missed her, and
wished she and Dad could have come to the wedding.

"Getting tired?" Tony asked from behind me.

"Sorry," I said, picking up my pace. "I was wool-gathering."

Shaking away the sadness, I looked up toward the cliffs, their layers of red and gold brilliant in the morning sun. They were easier to admire from this direction, and I could see some of the ranch buildings as well. Other trails crawled all over the hillsides, every which way. I spotted half a dozen other hikers scattered across the mesa on various trails.

By the time we reached the Staff House, I was ready for a big glass of something cold. We continued past it to the dining hall, where a few early-birds had lined up outside the cafeteria door, which was not yet open. In the dining hall itself, coffee and tea were always available. We walked on toward our room, and I sighed gratefully to be back inside, out of the sun. I splashed some cold water on my face and brushed my hair, then changed my boots for more comfortable sneakers.

A loud *thump* made me look up sharply. Tony was in the bathroom.

"Was that you?" I called.

He stepped out, frowning. "No."

A tinkle of distant laughter—a woman's laugh—made the frown deepen.

I tiptoed (as much as one can in boots) to the doorway of the second room. Outside the window on the south side, several people were listening to a tour guide. Two teens, a boy and a girl, were sitting at one of the patio tables, and the boy was leaning his chair back on two legs. Beyond them, a thin woman with straight, cropped auburn hair and a dour expression looked in through the window at me.

I pulled the door closed. Henceforth, I'd keep the curtains in that room drawn. I glanced toward the window by our bed. Those curtains were closed, but now I felt self-conscious.

"We *must* make the bed," I said.

Tony gave me a quizzical look. "You never just throw the covers over it? Even on weekends?"

"Humor me," I said, fluffing my pillow.

With two of us, it was easy to tidy the bed. I didn't insist on its being picture perfect, but as it was the most comfortable piece of furniture we had, I preferred that it be presentable. When I was satisfied, I picked up my purse and cautiously opened the door. The walking tour had progressed to the library, up the road. Tony and I locked our room and headed for the dining hall.

The line was now moving, and delicious smells emanated from

the kitchen. Lunch was green chile cheeseburgers, with a veggie burger option. I chose the real thing, and added a salad from the salad bar. Out on the condiments table were two kinds of dessert: chocolate pudding and Jell-o. There was also a soup bar in one corner of the hall that smelled interesting. Wishing there were trays, I served myself a bowl of tortilla soup and promised myself a dessert later. With hands full, I looked for a place to sit.

The football fan and his family were at the far end of the hall, near the wall of river rock. I could hear Football Fan's voice over all the other conversations in the room. He was debating the relative merits of the Texans and the Cowboys with the same middle-aged Anglo guy, who today was sporting a Cowboys T-shirt and a ball cap with an American flag on the front, worn backward over his buzz-cut.

Suppressing a wince at the violation of flag etiquette, not to mention everyday etiquette, I looked at Tony. "Want to sit outside?"

"Sure."

He opened the nearest door for me and I found a shady seat at one of the picnic tables on the long, south-facing *portal*. In summer time it might be too hot there at midday, but in January it was pretty pleasant. It was also blissfully quiet; the few other people outside kept their voices low.

Tony sat across from me. I glanced at his orange Jell-o and quirked an eyebrow.

"Don't judge," he said, and spooned up a bite right then.

"I'm not. Childhood favorite?"

"Oh, man, we lived on the stuff. Mama made two batches every day in summer time."

Jell-o was cheaper than ice cream. I kept that reflection to myself.

Tony had two sisters. I pictured his mother, a young widow, with two teens and an almost-teen to feed. It must have been tough.

I went back for a tall glass of iced tea, and picked up a bowl of chocolate pudding on my way back.

"Do you think your mom might like to do my hair for the wedding?" I said, as I settled in again.

Tony, who had just taken a huge bite of his burger, chewed thoughtfully for a while. "I know for a fact," he said when he'd swallowed, "that she's hoping you'll ask."

"Oh, good. I didn't want to presume, but I thought…"

"Yes. And don't even suggest paying her. She'd be offended."

"Well, OK."

The cheeseburgers were tasty enough, though not as good as Blake's. The soup was excellent. I ate my salad and drank my tea, enjoying the view and the peaceful atmosphere. Apart from the voices of those around me, the chatter of the birds in the trees, and the sound of an occasional car going by on the ranch road, it was beautifully quiet here. I felt myself relaxing. Something tight in my gut—of which I hadn't been aware—was slowly unwinding. It felt good.

I had finished my burger, salad, and soup, and was ready for pudding. "Think I'll get some coffee," I said. "Want anything?"

Tony shook his head, mouth full of Jell-o.

"Be right back."

I collected our empty dishes, leaving my pudding behind. Dropping the plates at the dishwashing window, I walked over to the coffee and tea station and encountered Mrs. Football Fan, who was browsing the teabags, pulling out each drawer and inspecting the bags in foil pouches, though the drawers were labeled with the varieties they contained. She was dressed in tight jeans, a pale gold sweater, and a long overshirt printed with black and white zig-zag designs in a vaguely tribal-looking style. She glanced up at me, and I gave her a smile.

"Not your favorite brand?"

She did a slight eyeroll. "Not even close," she said in a low voice. It wasn't a mumble; her diction was perfect, reinforcing my impression that her education had included substantial "polish."

"I'm a tea drinker, myself, usually, but coffee sounded good with chocolate pudding."

She turned an interested look on me. "Tea drinker?"

"Yes," I said as I filled a mug with coffee. "Actually, I brought a little kettle and some loose tea, so I could make it in my room."

"I wish I'd thought of that." She sighed as she selected a teabag, put it into her cup, and added hot water from the coffee machine. Steam rose from the cup, a good sign—most coffee makers didn't get water hot enough to brew tea.

"I could make you some, if you'd like," I said. "I brought plenty. I'm Ellen, by the way. Ellen Rosings."

Again the appraising gaze. "That's kind of you," she said, and set down her cup to offer a hand. "Lisette Roan."

"Nice to meet you," I said, shaking hands. Her grip was feather-light, her skin soft and a bit cold. I noticed her manicure was perfect: a subtly-frosted plum.

"Is this your first visit to New Mexico?" I asked.

She hesitated briefly, then said, simply, "Yes."

"Well, I hope you're enjoying it. And I meant it about the tea. I'd be happy to make you some."

"Perhaps later." She gave me a brief smile, then picked up her cup and walked toward the back of the hall.

Standoffish, or just shy? I knew I sometimes gave the impression of snobbery when I was simply feeling timid. I took my coffee back to the *portal*, where Tony was looking at his phone.

"Expecting a call?"

He looked up as I resumed my seat. "Nah, just killing time."

"You're not bored, are you?"

"No." He put the phone down and made a show of admiring the view.

I ate a bite of pudding. It was made fresh, not spooned from a can, and tasted as wonderful as chocolate pudding could be without being *pot de crème*. A sip of coffee complemented it nicely.

"Good food here," I remarked.

"Yeah. Not fancy, but good."

A burst of shouting from inside the dining hall had Tony on his feet in a second. He went to the nearest window, then his tense stance relaxed.

"It's that guy—"

"Football Fan?"

"Uh-huh."

Tony remained at the window, still on half-alert, listening. The voices argued on, but at a lower volume. Finally a stomping tread preceded the emergence of the guy with the execrable flag hat, his face nearly as red as the stripes, from the door at the end of the hall. He continued to the road, where his angry steps raised little puffs of dust.

Tony's eyes narrowed as he watched, and I wondered what he was thinking. Determining the likelihood that the guy was armed? Evaluating risk of violence?

Sympathizing?

I sighed, turning back to my dessert. The coffee was now lukewarm, and I drank a big swallow before it got any colder. I savored the last of the pudding, then got up to take my dishes inside.

Tony came back to the table. "I'll get that," he said, taking the pudding bowl and stacking it with his empty Jell-o bowl. He held out a hand for my coffee cup, but I kept it.

"I'm getting seconds," I said.

Tony frowned, opened his mouth, then shut it again and headed into the hall, keeping in front of me.

Oh, my. Was this chivalry? Kind of gave me a warm feeling.

I glanced toward the back of the room. Football Fan has settled down, now that his shouting partner was gone. No doubt everyone in the room was relieved.

I glimpsed his wife—Lisette, I reminded myself—saying something to her son, who was seated beside her. Too far away to read her expression, but her body language was tight, controlled.

I fetched myself a half-cup of coffee and gulped it down, since Tony was waiting on me. I wanted the caffeine, because I felt inclined to take a siesta, and I knew we didn't have time.

"When do we need to check in for the tour?" Tony asked as we headed back to our room.

"Twelve forty-five."

Roughly half an hour. The bus would pick us up at the Georgia O'Keeffe Welcome Center by the Abiquiu Inn. The drive over there wouldn't take long; we had a few minutes to relax. I sat on the bed and glanced at my phone in case there were any urgent messages. There weren't, so I put it down and lay back. Then I got up, went to the Room of Many Chairs and closed all the curtains before returning to the bed.

Tony took out his phone and looked at it, then glanced at me and put it back in his pocket. He started pacing the room. I watched him for a minute, then decided to offer him some diversion.

"Want to go a little early and look at the gift shop?"

"Sure," he said.

I collected the tickets I had printed out, tucked them into my purse, and decided to leave my sweater behind. It was a pleasant day, and we'd be inside for a lot of the tour. My long-sleeved shirt would be warm enough.

We locked up and hopped in the car, and in a few minutes we pulled into the parking lot at the Abiquiu Inn. Quite a few cars were there, but I found the last empty parking space near the welcome center and tucked my car into it.

The Georgia O'Keeffe Welcome Center—a giant, gray cube of a structure—could not have been more different than the sprawling adobe complex of the Inn. Though it was winter, the bare-branched cottonwood trees still provided a soft backdrop for the Inn. The welcome center had no such visual relief.

We went in and gave our names to the receptionist, who invited us to watch a short film about O'Keeffe in a small room off the lobby. Tony shrugged when I asked if he wanted to see it, which I interpreted as interest that was marginal at best. He was looking at his phone, scrolling the screen, by which I deduced that there was cell connectivity here.

"Let's look at the shop first," I said.

The gift shop was full of books, posters, calendars, little gifty-things, and of course, prints of O'Keeffe's artwork. I browsed the books, and looked over a shelf of dishes including teapots, along with a stack of square canisters of tea labeled "Hu-Kwa," which rang a bell. I picked one up and looked more closely; ah, yes—a famous Lapsang Souchong. I considered getting a canister for Kris, filed it under "maybe," and continued browsing. If I bought anything, I would wait until we got back so I didn't have to carry a package around on the tour.

Tony had settled by the books, and was looking at his phone again. I pretended not to notice.

The entertaining aspects of the gift shop exhausted, I collected Tony and headed back to the lobby, where we admired some historic photos displayed on the walls, and poked our heads briefly into the movie room. By then, it was almost time to get on the bus, and I drifted toward the front doors with Tony in my wake. Before I got there, the doors burst open and in came Football Fan and family.

"Where's the damn bus?" said Football Fan in a voice that filled the cavernous lobby. He stormed toward the reception desk, followed closely by Lisette and at a distance by their son, wearing earbuds and staring at his phone as he shuffled after them.

Football Fan began a loud complaint, but Lisette swiftly intervened, and the murmuring voices that followed were indistinguishable. I looked at Tony and found him watching me.

"Oh, boy," he said.

I sighed.

My faint hope that Football Fan was just escorting his family to the tour rendezvous and wouldn't actually be accompanying them evaporated when he pushed his way to the front of the line as the small tour bus arrived. Lisette shot me a glance as she followed, half apologetic, half defiant. Resigned, I boarded the bus and took the farthest seat possible from the family, which put me and Tony at the back of the bus.

Tony seemed not to care. He was already resigned to a couple of hours of boredom, I supposed. I, on the other hand, had been looking forward to this tour, and hoped my enjoyment of it wouldn't be ruined.

Another dozen or so people joined us, filling the bus. I relaxed a bit when it was full, and realized I'd been bracing for the guy with the flag hat to arrive and complete my joy.

The tour guide stood at the front and began his narration as the driver pulled onto the highway. The drive was short, less than a mile to the turnoff that led to the tiny village of Abiquiu proper. The bus swung sharply around and climbed a steep hill. The guide grabbed a support pole and continued talking without missing a beat. He must have done this many times.

Adobe walls hid most of the buildings from view. We passed the village church, which was in the traditional Spanish mission style and impressively large. No doubt many of the parishioners lived in the surrounding hills and the river valley.

The bus drove through a gate in an adobe wall and into a large parking lot. Gardens to the south, enclosed by more walls, were almost as large as O'Keeffe's home itself, a sprawling group of single-story adobe structures perched atop the bluff overlooking the Chama River valley. I'd read in the O'Keeffe biography that it had once been a convent, and had been long disused when O'Keeffe first sought to buy it from the church, a negotiation that had taken a while.

We left the bus and gathered around while the guide talked about the architecture. Football Fan's son was still absorbed in his phone, until his father gave him a buffet on the shoulder and ordered him to put it away. This struck me as unlike the father, and I looked for Lisette, wondering if she had asked him to intervene. From her frown, I gathered not.

I was frowning too, I realized. That buffet had been close to a blow. The boy now looked sulky; the glance he shot his father edged with fear.

Disturbing, but none of my business. Nothing had occurred that merited a stranger's intervention. I shook it off and returned my attention to the guide as he led us into the garden.

"The water comes from the village's *acequia*," he told us, pointing out the small irrigation ditches—more like brick-lined troughs, really—that ran through the vegetable plots and a small orchard. The gardens were impressive. I knew from the book that O'Keeffe had planted them because she'd grown tired of eating canned fruits and vegetables, and because traveling to a grocery in Santa Fe had been unreliable in winter.

How different things were now. Santa Fe was an easy drive today; only the most extreme weather could interfere with travel along the paved roads that had not existed when O'Keeffe came to live here.

The guide led us through a doorway into an enclosed patio, and suddenly we were standing in an O'Keeffe painting. Several paintings, rather—she had painted this place many times. The guide pointed out the small, squarish door that had featured in a number of the paintings—according to one quote, O'Keeffe said she'd bought the house because of that door.

I gazed at that side of the building, taking in the straight lines of roof and walls, the stepping stones that had become abstract little squares in at least one painting, the bright blue of the sky above the pale brown adobe. Of course such sights would appeal to an artist.

For a moment I wished I had brought Julio with me. Maybe I'd give him a gift of this tour, if he seemed interested. He had painted Vi for me, after all.

In the center of the patio stood *Abstraction*, a large and famous sculpture O'Keeffe had created in her later years, when failing eyesight had limited her ability to paint. Several castings existed.

After giving us a few minutes to take in the patio, and take photos, which were allowed outside but not inside the house, the tour guide shepherded us indoors. The house had been restored to its condition when O'Keeffe had left it, with furnishings and fixtures preserved. Rocks that she had collected on hikes and journeys lined the windowsills. The dining table she had designed —little more than a long plank of wood resting on sawhorses— stood beneath the large, white globe of a Japanese lantern, the gift of a friend.

In the pantry and kitchen, jars of herbs and goods from the garden lined shelves to the ceiling. Several teapots stood on one shelf, and I commented aloud on them.

"Yes, O'Keeffe preferred tea to coffee," said the guide. "She drank it every evening. This was her favorite kind; she had it imported especially." He gestured to a canister of Lapsang Souchong like the ones in the gift shop.

Aha! Well, now I *had* to buy some.

Lisette caught my eye across the room and smiled. I smiled back. She seemed more relaxed now, and I realized her husband and son were no longer with us. I verified this by looking at everyone in the group: two couples—one older, one young and Hispanic, three middle-aged white women who appeared to be together, a tall, thin, silent man who reminded me a little of my neighbor Bob Hutchins, and a solitary woman with short hair of a dullish red-brown who looked rather familiar. Maybe I'd seen her in the dining hall at Ghost Ranch.

If I knew Tony, he had probably noticed Football Fan's absence as well. He seemed unconcerned, so I dismissed a worry that father and son had ventured into some room where we weren't allowed to go. No doubt the tour guide would be on watch for such transgressions.

A workroom beyond the kitchen was long and low-ceilinged, filled with indirect light from large, north-facing windows. White geraniums and a large jade plant stood by these, enjoying the daylight.

"This plant is descended from one that O'Keeffe kept here. After she moved to Santa Fe, that plant died of neglect, but her dear friend and assistant Juan Hamilton saved some cuttings and started new ones. This came from one of those cuttings, and you can get plants started from this one in the gift shop."

Ka-ching. I *had* to have a jade plant descended from O'Keeffe's. I wondered if they were selling geraniums, too.

The guide led us outside into another little garden, this one for pleasure rather than produce. To the north stood another adobe building, which the guide invited us to enter through a narrow doorway. This, he told us proudly, was O'Keeffe's studio.

Beyond a short entryway, the building opened out into a long room with huge picture windows to the north, the giant cousin of the sunny kitchen workroom. The indirect light would be an artist's dream, and the view of the Chama River valley, with long bluffs to the west and the river *bosque* below, was breathtaking. Even without leaves, the trees of the *bosque* had a ghostly beauty. In summer, and especially in autumn when the cottonwoods would turn golden, they must be stunning.

More rocks along the window sills here, and just outside stood a large wooden stump also covered with rocks. The guide pointed out work tables where O'Keeffe framed her pictures, and tools she had used. I was less interested in these than in the room itself and its sparse furnishings, which included a lounge chair of a particular style that she had preferred. A small sculpture—another of her famous works, this one early—stood on a glass coffee table.

The guide pointed out O'Keeffe's private bedroom through a small doorway to the east, but did not allow us to go in. Instead he led us outside, past the rock-covered stump, along the windows to one that looked into the small bedroom. More rocks and a few bits of art were the only decoration. She had pared her life down to necessities, and while she didn't stint on her own comfort, there were very few superfluous objects in the house.

The little bedroom was a bit of a let-down—a small finish to an extraordinary place. Such was life, however; in her final years, O'Keeffe had produced less and less art. She had moved to Santa Fe not because it was (by then) a center of the Southwestern art world, but in order to be closer to medical care.

The tour was over. I stood looking out over the valley, smelling the familiar scent of sun-baked New Mexico soil and the evergreen esters of piñon and juniper. What a life this remarkable woman had led, much of it in defiance of convention. She had done things that women like myself now took for granted—living alone, conducting her own business, not to mention her ambition to be an artist—but when she had done them she'd been a rebel.

The guide made his final remarks, then headed for the waiting bus, leaving us to return in our own time. Tony joined me and looked over the valley.

"Enjoy it?" he asked.

"Oh, yes! I hope you weren't bored."

"No—it was interesting."

I smiled. "I noticed you weren't glued to your phone."

"Yeah, well—no bars up here."

I verified this by taking out my own phone, then shot a few pictures of the valley and the house. I wanted some durable memories of this lovely, interesting day. Hoping to get a picture of the gardens, because I hadn't been taking pictures at the beginning of the tour, I strolled back to the gate and snapped a few over the wall. Gazing into the oasis of green, I pictured O'Keeffe walking through the orchard, picking an apricot or a plum from the trees.

A familiar loud voice jarred me out of my reverie.

"Get on that bus! You're lucky I don't ground your ass!"

Football Fan and his son were coming toward us from the village end of the parking lot. The boy protested, "I didn't go in there until you did!"

"Yeah, but you the one got us kicked out!"

"But the sign said—"

Football Fan aimed a clout at his son. This time the boy ducked. His father grabbed him by his jacket and shoved him forward, almost pushing him into Tony.

"Out of the way, Pedro," the man said, glowering.

My heart stood still for a second. Tony, stone-faced, stood his ground. Football Fan frowned, but pulled his son away, propelling him toward the bus.

I exhaled in relief, looking at Tony. There was cold fury in his eyes, then he noticed me and shook it off.

"Jerk," he said, turning his back on the bus.

I looked for Lisette. She was hurrying toward the bus, a stricken expression on her face.

Anger settled in the pit of my stomach; I was certain now that Football Fan was physically abusive toward his child.

Most of the others on the tour had already boarded the bus. The few who remained wore grim faces; they had noted Football Fan's behavior. The short-haired woman gazed after Lisette with narrowed eyes, her mouth a thin line. Tony and I boarded, brushing past Football Fan who had claimed the front row, supposedly reserved for handicapped passengers. We found seats in the back, and soon the bus started off on the brief journey back to the welcome center.

The tour guide gave us a wrap-up speech during the drive. I confess it didn't register; I was worrying about the boy and his mother. Nothing I could do, except continue to be vigilant. Tony openly watched the father and son, sharing the front row while Lisette had taken a seat in the row behind them. Except for once leaning forward to say something in a low voice to her husband, who ignored her, she sat rigidly silent.

The family were first off the bus, and to my relief they headed for the parking lot rather than going into the welcome center. I returned to the gift shop and collected two tins of O'Keeffe's favorite tea and a tiny jade plant: no more than a couple of leaves in a little two-inch pot; no wonder I hadn't noticed them the first time. It being January, the calendars were all on sale. I waffled between a wall calendar and a weekly planner, then decided to get both. What the heck. They were discounted, and filled with beautiful O'Keeffe art. In fact, I grabbed a second planner as a gift for Nat, then carried my haul up to the register to check out. The clerk put my purchases into an elegant gray cloth shopping bag and tucked some tissue paper around the jade plant's pot to protect it.

Tony was waiting in the lobby, and swiftly pocketed his phone as I emerged from the gift shop.

"You're allowed to look at your phone," I said.

"I'd rather look at you," he said, taking the bag out of my hand.

"Thanks." I dug my keys out of my pocket and unlocked the car. "Would you mind keeping hold of that so it doesn't tip over? There's a plant in there."

Tony peered into the bag. "OK."

He tucked it between his feet in the foot well. I drove back to Ghost Ranch at a leisurely pace. The dashboard clock said 2:37. I'd have time to relax with some tea, unless Tony was hot for another hike. I hoped he wasn't; it was warmer now, and I was a little tired.

"Mind if I leave you alone for a couple hours?" he asked as I parked the car. "There's a game on."

I smiled. "Not at all. You sussed out a TV?"

"There's one in the cantina," he said, gesturing up the road. "It's just past the dining hall."

"A cantina? That's a surprise! Does it have a bar?"

"I think it's more of a meeting room, actually," Tony said. "This place doesn't have any bars."

"Of any kind," I added.

"Ha, ha." Tony unlocked our room. "Do you want to come, too?"

I shook my head. "Not really a football fan. Speaking of which —if that man is there…"

"Don't worry. He's not worth the trouble," Tony assured me, though he looked a bit stony. "You sure you won't be bored?"

I lifted the shopping bag. "I have amusements. And I might take a shower."

"Great." He tossed his hat onto the dresser, then caught me around the waist.

I hastily set down the bag so I could return his embrace. He kissed me breathless, grinned, and headed for the door. "See you in a bit."

"Have fun," I called as the door closed.

Football.

I shrugged. It was good to have some alone time. We really didn't need to be joined at the hip.

Really. We didn't.

Come on, Ellen. Who was just wishing for some down time?

It was partly worry. Football Fan had offered Tony a pretty bald insult, and I knew how angry Tony could get. But I had to trust him. He had excellent discipline, I reminded myself. He'd be all right.

I put the kettle on and spread my purchases out on the bed, admiring them. I wasn't sure how much water jade trees liked—I'd have to look it up—but the soil seemed awfully dry so I gave it a little water and set it on a chair in the Room of Many Chairs, saving the tissue paper for the trip home.

Should I brew some of the Lapsang Souchong? I decided I wasn't up for it, and instead got out the little tin of Assam that I'd brought. Lemon would have made it a perfect afternoon refreshment, but alas I had only a bit of raw sugar.

I hadn't noticed any lemon in the dining hall. There was the snack bar in the visitor center; maybe I could snag a slice of lemon there. I turned off the kettle, which hadn't yet boiled, and grabbed my sweater.

A path led between the south side of the Ghost House and the O'Keeffe Cottage (even smaller than the Ghost House), up the hill toward some of the other "casitas" and older ranch buildings, and along the hilltop to the welcome center. I thought that would be preferable to walking down the road and up the long, uneven steps. As I came around the west side of the Ghost House, where the public entrance was, I decided to go inside just for a minute.

While the walled courtyard was spacious, this part of the old house, just like our part, was small, with narrow, rectangular rooms and thick adobe walls. The main room was the largest, and probably the oldest. To the south, with a step down, was a smaller room with its long dimension at right angles to the main room. In one corner was a kiva fireplace, blocked. Maybe the only fireplace on the ranch that wasn't blocked was the one in the dining hall.

I went back to the main room, where the walls were covered with historic photos of various buildings around the ranch and of Arthur and Phoebe Pack, early owners who had made Ghost Ranch a successful dude ranch and eventually left it to the Presbyterian Church. I did not read all of the captions, but those I read enlightened me somewhat.

The Packs were not the first owners. In fact, the first people to live on the ranch land were the Archuleta brothers, who had built the adobe house I was standing in, and who had been notorious for rustling cattle.

Charming.

I glanced at the other captions, looking for an explanation of the Ghost House's name, but didn't find one. I decided this was enough history for now. I wanted my tea.

Emerging, I looked eastward across the courtyard wall, toward the big, open field. If there had been many children here I would have expected to see them playing there, but Lisette's boy was the only child I had seen at the ranch. I wondered if he liked football.

The Superbowl was coming up, wasn't it? So the games this month would be exciting and important to enthusiasts. Of whom my fiancé was apparently one.

Beyond the field were two long, single-story buildings that I recognized. The one on the north end was the Staff House, where Tony and I had found the trailhead for our hike. As I looked at it, a man in cowboy duds came out of the building. He was not the red-headed cowboy; he was a little shorter, a little more barrel-chested. I couldn't tell at that distance, but something about his shape made me think he was the redhead's partner. He started toward me, which made me nervous until I remembered the map, which showed the stables west of the welcome center.

Welcome center, yes. I hastened up the path, and saw that it branched. One side continued up to a small parking lot surrounded by several casitas, each with more than one door. I followed the other branch to the left and along the hilltop to the main building.

The snack bar was closed, and I saw no sign of lemon there. In the dining area, which had some wrought-iron patio furniture, was a widescreen TV against the wall, playing a video about Ghost Ranch for an absent audience.

The trading post was open, staffed by a solitary cashier—an older man in a plaid shirt and jeans, bored and maybe a little sulky at having to work during The Game, which was playing without volume on a small TV by the register. The shop's only other occupant was Lisette Roan, standing in front of a rack of chips and candy, staring blankly at the array.

I JOINED HER. "Looking for an energy boost?"

She looked at me, surprised, then embarrassed. "Oh. Well, I wanted to get something for my son."

I nodded. She seemed uncomfortable, so I stepped away toward a refrigerated case filled with drinks. There were half-pints of chocolate milk, and a solitary plain milk. I snagged it, figuring buying it would be quicker than walking back to the dining hall.

Lisette was still staring numbly at the carbohydrates. I gave a little cough.

"I'm about to make some tea, if you'd like some."

"Oh, I—" She started to shake her head, and brushed at her cheek. "Th-that's nice of you."

"You'd be doing me a favor," I added, only slightly exaggerating. "I'd love some company. My fiancé's gone off to watch a football game."

Lisette winced, then her jaw stiffened and she drew herself up like a queen. "Yes, well. Thank you, a cup of tea would be lovely."

I remembered that I had only one mug in the room, so I picked out a souvenir mug with O'Keeffe's cow-skull design and paid for it and the milk. Leading Lisette back to my room, I set an easy pace, since her wedge-heeled sandals were more fashionable than practical and the footing on the path was uneven. I didn't make conversation, figuring that she could use some quiet to regain her composure. By the time we reached the Ghost House, she seemed calmer.

I opened the door to our room and held it for her. She glanced around the room before stepping in. A cautious habit? Worthy of

Tony, I thought. Glad that I'd insisted on making the bed, I led her through to the Room of Many Chairs.

"Make yourself at home," I said, turning on the light and picking up my kettle. "Choose your favorite chair. Do you prefer Darjeeling or Assam?"

Standing in the middle of all the chairs, looking slightly bewildered, she glanced at me over her shoulder.

"Darjeeling, I guess."

I smiled. "I'll be right back."

I washed the new mug in the bathroom sink, filled the kettle, and returned to set it heating. Lisette had chosen a sturdy chair with a carved wooden back and a padded seat. I took a nearby chair, leaving one between us for a table.

"I've also got some Lapsang Souchong, if you'd like that," I said.

"No, thanks. Too heavy."

I nodded. "I only drink it occasionally, myself, but my office manager loves it."

That evoked a curious glance. "Office manager? You're an entrepreneur?"

"Yes. I own a restaurant. Well, a tearoom, actually."

"A tearoom! No wonder you brought your own."

I smiled. "I'm afraid I'm a bit of a tea snob."

That got a laugh out of her, and the first smile I'd seen from her since the studio tour. "If you're a tea snob, may I join your club?"

"Absolutely. It's open to all."

The kettle was emitting some steam. I checked, and it was just short of boiling, perfect for Darjeeling. I poured the steaming water over the leaves, then set the teapot's lid on top of the infuser while it steeped.

"Do you take milk?" I asked.

"No, but I'm glad you do," Lisette said, with the first smile I'd seen from her since the tour. "Or you wouldn't have come to the trading post, would you? Oh, and I forgot to get Jeremy a treat!"

"Jeremy? Is that your son?"

"Yes. He's off with his father, watching football."

Lucky Tony. Maybe they'd be engrossed in the game.

"How old is he?" I asked.

"Eleven."

"Do you have other children?"

She shook her head, and something—sadness, anger?—tightened her face before the finishing-school calm returned. No more family questions, then.

My timer went off. I offered sugar and milk, which Lisette declined. I put a dollop of milk into my mug and handed the souvenir mug to her. Sipping carefully, I leaned back in my chair.

Ah, tea. A nice hot cuppa after a busy day.

Lisette echoed my contentment with a small sigh. "Thank you. This is lovely."

"Have you been a tea enthusiast for long?"

The smile returned. "My Auntie Rachelle always had tea in the afternoon. A proper tea with something to eat, even if it was only bread and butter. In the summer she'd make iced tea for me, but she always had hers hot."

I wondered if Auntie Rachelle was behind Lisette's polish. "Where was this?"

"Houston."

"Is that still home?"

She nodded. "All my life, except for college."

"Where'd you go for that?" I asked.

"Tulane for my bachelor's, and then I got a scholarship to the Art Institute of Chicago."

"So you're an artist?"

"Yes."

And that was why the family was here. O'Keeffe had spent some time at the Art Institute of Chicago, according to the biography I was reading. Doubtless a talented, strong-willed woman like Lisette would be drawn to her example.

"How did you like the studio tour?" I asked.

Her eyes lit with delight. "It was wonderful, don't you think? That workroom, with those views! What a glorious place to live and work!"

"Glorious and isolated," I mused.

"Even better."

She took a sip of tea. The sadness had crept back.

"I guess all artists need a lot of alone time," I said. "I need it myself, and I'm no artist."

"I haven't painted since I got married."

Whoa. Unable to think of a response, I held still. Lisette

turned her mug in her hands, then took a deep swallow, not a ladylike sip.

"I thought I'd made a great bargain. Wesley has money, you see. Lots of money." She glanced at me, then drank again. "I thought I'd be free to make art, and he'd support me. I mean really support me—be my advocate. But he doesn't care about art. He just wanted a pretty wife."

I swallowed. What could I say? What would Miss Manners say? Holy moly!

"You saw how he treated Jeremy. And he loves that child." Her tone was unmistakably bitter.

"I'm so sorry," I whispered. "Is there anything...?"

She shook her head, straightened in the chair, and finished her tea. "I shouldn't have bothered you with it. Nothing anyone can do."

"Do you...have a place you can go? I mean—"

"Auntie Rachelle's. Wesley's afraid of her. She's getting old, but she can still give him what for."

"Oh."

"Sometimes I say she's sick and I have to take care of her for a few days. But really it's the other way around." Her voice broke on the last word and she wiped at her eyes with one elegant hand.

"I wish I could help," I said.

"Thanks." She drew an unsteady breath, and flashed a brave smile. "You have. Thanks for listening. I know I can rely on your discretion."

"I'm not sure how you know that, but thank you."

"You're a kind person. And you have discerning taste." She raised her mug with a wry smile.

Mine was also empty. "I think we need another round, yes?" I said, standing.

"Yes, please."

She held out her mug. I filled it from the teapot, which left half a mug for me. Lisette stood and walked over to the south window, pushed back the curtain to look out.

How soon had she discovered her mistake? I wondered. Before her son was born?

"Why is this called the 'Ghost House'?" she asked.

"I wish I knew. The brochure doesn't explain, and the people I've asked didn't know or wouldn't say. Either the story is unsavory, or it's shrouded in the mists of time."

She laughed softly and let the curtain fall. "Or it's a fabrication, for marketing purposes."

I tilted my head. "I don't know. Ghost Ranch has been the name of this place for a long time. There's probably *something* behind it."

"Does it make you afraid to stay here?" she asked, gesturing to the room.

Surprised by the question, I said, "Ah—no."

"You're brave."

"Well, my tearoom has a resident ghost. A very nice one, fortunately."

She turned to me, eyes wide. "A *ghost?* Really?"

I nodded.

"Well, now I have to bring Jeremy. He would *love* to see a ghost!"

"Actually, nobody's seen him. Not even me. He likes to turn on lights, play the piano, that sort of thing."

Lisette blinked. "Well, that's still pretty good. Where is your tearoom?"

"Santa Fe."

"Oh! We're going there after this weekend. I insisted we should see either Taos or Santa Fe on this trip."

She came back to her chair. I sipped my tea.

"Why not both?"

"I wanted both, but Wesley drew the line at one or the other. So I opted for Santa Fe and Canyon Road."

"Good choice," I said. "But I'm biased, of course."

That drew a chuckle from her. She seemed to be regaining her balance.

"It's more cosmopolitan, too, and that's better for Wesley," she said. "I haven't been to Taos, but I heard it's mostly whites and Mexicans."

I paused, then decided she hadn't meant to be offensive. "And Puebloans," I added, feeling culturally sensitive.

"'Damn Indians,' Wesley calls them."

I couldn't help giving her a shocked look. "Um, they were there first."

"Sorry. That's what Wesley says—it's not how *I* feel. I've never met an Indian."

I gazed at her, wondering how such a sophisticated woman could have such big blind spots. But then, we all have them. We just don't know about them until we're confronted with them. I thought back ruefully to my first encounters with Tony—still less than a year ago—which had been far from pleasant. He and I had both learned a lot from each other—and no doubt would learn more—about tolerance and acceptance. And I'd had rather a shock in coming to grips with the privileges I had taken for granted all my life.

Maybe Lisette had a little of that going on. Perhaps she had a blind spot about Indians purely due to lack of exposure. One might think that being black would make her more sensitive to injustice, but I didn't know her whole background. If she had grown up with money, she might have huge blind spots. If she hadn't—then maybe her marriage had been a decision to lower her expectations in exchange for security. And maybe lowered expectations had come with unpleasant attitudes.

Bargains. We made bargains all the time—with ourselves, with each other, with life.

Lisette was from Houston. Texas had plenty of Hispanics, most of whom were technically Chicanos (mostly Mexican Indian rather than the pureblood Spanish implied by the term Hispanic). It was the same in New Mexico, but cultural pride insisted on Hispanic as the preferred term, and I wasn't one to flout cultural pride. I wondered how Lisette felt about Hispanics, or Mexicans as she'd called them. If I introduced her to Tony, how would she react?

No sense pondering. Better to invite her to expand her horizons.

"There's a musician from Taos Pueblo playing a concert here tonight," I said. "Are you going?"

"I hadn't planned to, but…Wesley will be watching football."

"Come to the concert, then," I said.

"Maybe I will."

I'd finished my tea. I put my mug on the chair between us.

"Don't answer this if it's too nosy," I said, "but how did you convince your husband to come here?"

She sighed. "I talked him into it because of the trail ride. Jeremy loves horses."

"Oh. Did you enjoy that?"

She sipped her tea. "Haven't done it yet. We're going tomorrow morning."

Oh, joy. A trail ride with Football Fan.

"We're taking the same tour again, then," I said, making sure to smile. "Should be fun."

"Do you like riding horses?" she asked.

"Haven't been in the saddle since summer camp, but I loved it then."

Summer camp, up in the mountains. Rich white kids from Texas, with their shiny black riding boots and black velvet helmets. Me with my scruffy cowboy boots and straw cowboy hat. In my embarrassment, I'd failed to perceive my own privilege. There were no black kids at that camp. Maybe no Hispanics, either. I frowned, trying to remember.

The African American population of New Mexico had never been high, for various reasons, including the fact that slavery had never been legal here. There were more blacks since Katrina, when we had an influx of refugees from New Orleans, but even so they were less than five percent of the state's population. And the animosity between blacks and Hispanics in New Mexico was legendary. I wondered if that had inspired Lisette's remark about whites and Mexicans, and her husband's rudeness to Tony.

"I've only been riding a couple of times," Lisette said. "I'm not good at it. And Wesley's never been, but he's too stubborn to admit it. He wants to impress Jeremy."

I smiled. "Don't worry. Tours like this, the horses are very gentle, and the guides keep an eye out. You'll be fine."

"I'd rather go on the bus, to be honest. But the trail ride's what got me here." She sighed. "I thought seeing O'Keeffe's country—the places she painted—would give me a jump start."

I tilted my head. "There are pastels and colored pencils in that trading post, you know. And drawing paper. Watercolors, too, I think."

"I paint in oils," Lisette said haughtily.

I shrugged. "Maybe a little sketching would be a good warm-up."

She looked at me, then at her mug. "Sorry. I guess I'm in a funk."

"It's OK."

We sat in silence for a while. I watched Lisette, wondering

how she had decided on her particular bargain. Was Wesley the best she could do?

I would probably never know the answers.

"I should go," she said, setting down her empty mug. "Thank you again—and I'm terribly sorry, but would you remind me of your name?"

I smiled. "It's Ellen. Don't worry, I'm pretty sad at remembering names, too."

"Ellen. Thank you, for the tea, and for your patience."

"My pleasure," I said, standing and going over to the table chair. "I made you up a couple of tea bags, for later." I held them out to her. "And this is my card. If you have time when you get to Santa Fe, look me up and I'll treat you to afternoon tea."

"Thank you!" She smiled as she examined my card. "Wisteria Tearoom. Auntie Rachelle has a wisteria vine on her porch!"

"They're wonderful aren't they?"

"Yes. And I *will* look you up, but we'll pay for our tea." She gave me a wry grin. "Wesley can afford it!"

"Will he enjoy it?" I asked doubtfully.

"Probably not, but I will. And it'll be good for Jeremy."

"You're a good mom, giving him new experiences."

She surprised me with a fierce look. "He's going to have better prospects than his father. I'm making sure of that."

I walked with her to the door. "See you later at the concert?"

"Maybe. If I'm not busy." She straightened her shoulders. "I'm going to go back to that trading post and get some pastels."

I smiled. "Then I hope you'll be too busy for the concert."

"Thank you, Ellen." She gave me a quick hug. "Thank you."

"You're welcome, Lisette."

I watched her walk up the path, toward the welcome center. Closing the door, I looked around our modest room.

Modest by my standards. Luxurious for others. Everyone had their own perspective.

This day had given me plenty of food for thought. A hot shower would give me a chance to chew on it.

I was in the Room of Many Chairs, reading my O'Keeffe biography, when Tony returned. He came in whistling, grinned, and came over to pull me up out of my chair. I barely had time to set my bookmark.

"I gather your team won," I said, as he covered my face in kisses.

"Uh-huh." He picked me up and carried me toward the bed.

"Ah—it's almost time for dinner," I said.

"It can wait." He laid me on the bed and proceeded to make me tingle in all kinds of delightful ways, stroking his hands along my body.

"But there's the concert—"

"You hungry?" he asked, his breath tickling my ear.

"Yes, as a matter of fact." Although he was presenting a serious challenge to my priorities.

"Me, too."

His hands found the button on my jeans and expertly unfastened it.

We were late for dinner.

The dining hall was even louder than it had been at breakfast, though there weren't more than about thirty people. Football Fan —Wesley—was at it again, arguing loudly with anyone who got within range. He seemed in a foul mood, and I deduced that his team had lost the afternoon game. Jeremy, seated next to his father, had withdrawn into his phone, hunched over it with his earbuds in. I didn't see Lisette.

Tony and I carried our plates of enchilada casserole outside, and watched the clouds over the mountains turn pink in the setting sun's last light. To the west, rays of golden white poured through gaps in the clouds, making "glories," as my mother had called them. Maybe Lisette was capturing them on paper.

"You don't have to come to the concert," I told Tony. "I know there's another game on."

"Eh, not one I care about. I'll come with you."

"Thank you," I said primly.

He grinned. "I'd come even if I cared about the game. You've got priority."

"Do I? That's lovely."

"Too many stray stallions around here," he added, his gaze following a couple of men in western shirts and chaps who had just emerged from the dining hall, carrying plates. It was the red-headed guy and his friend. The latter shot me a look over his shoulder, but looked away again quickly. They chose a table a couple down from ours, and sat with weary sighs.

"Why, Tony! Are you jealous?"

"Of them? Pfft."

I laughed. "You're right. No contest."

He took my hand, his dark eyes intense. We sat like that for a moment. Memories of our recent pleasure echoed through my body.

I watched the sky as I ate my enchiladas. The clouds to the east were now edged with raspberry, and the glories had gone from the west. The sun was playing hide-and-seek with the western clouds as it sank. A cold breeze blew by. Once the sun was down, it would swiftly get cold. I was glad I had brought my coat.

"When do we have to be there?" Tony asked.

"Seven. We've got time for dessert if you like. That apple pie looked good."

"Yeah. Can I bring you a piece?"

"Please. Shall I get us some coffee?"

"That would be great. Meet you back here."

He squeezed my hand, then headed inside. I could feel the attention of the two wranglers as soon as he was gone. Ignoring them, I stood and was about to go in for the coffee when I heard a car engine roaring nearby, coming up the road from the direction of the visitor center. There were signs all over saying not to drive beyond such and such a point, but this vehicle—a dusty Jeep that might once have been red—ignored them all and drove straight up to the dining hall. It stopped, coughed once, and fell still even as a wiry man with gray hair (sticking out every which way from beneath a battered ball cap) and a bushy gray beard jumped out and marched toward me.

"Told you once I told you a million times. Stay the hell offa my property!"

6

I BLINKED, FEELING LIKE A FAWN CAUGHT IN HEADLIGHTS, then realized he was not addressing me. He marched past without noticing me, up to the table where the two cowboys sat.

"We didn't go on your property, Ezra," said the redhead.

"You came right up to the fence!" Ezra continued at full volume, making me wonder if he might be deaf. His clothes hung on him, as if he'd lost weight in the decade or so since he'd bought them, making him look scarecrowish.

"That's where the trail runs," said the redhead patiently.

"And any one of your fool tourists could ride right through that gap by the arroyah!" The old man spat for emphasis.

"Well, maybe you should mend your fence."

This suggestion apparently made Ezra's brain explode. His answer was loud and garbled, and I couldn't decipher it. Tony returned about halfway through it.

"What's up?" he asked, setting a piece of pie in front of me.

"Neighborly dispute, I think."

Tony glanced at the table where the redhead was now speaking in low tones to Ezra, who stood with arms folded and jaw out-thrust. "Great. I think those guys are the trail ride guides."

"I think so, too. That gentleman is, um, reminding them to keep the tourists on the trail."

Tony rolled his eyes, sat down, and dug into his pie. I went and fetched our coffee, then sat down to enjoy my pie. It was excellent, although the crust wasn't as good as Julio's. After a few minutes, Ezra stomped away, got back in his Jeep, and drove off, with unnecessary speed and volume.

"Didn't realize this vacation included a free soap opera," Tony remarked. "Between these guys and the football a—aficionado… can't get away from it."

I chuckled, glancing at the cowboys. The Hispanic one was glowering over his shoulder at the departing Jeep and its dust cloud.

"Humans," I said, quoting Kris. "Hey, I've never heard you say 'aficionado' before."

"Learned it from you. How'd I do?"

"Beautifully. And very diplomatic."

Tony laughed and ate the last of his pie. We took our dishes in, then walked across the road to the Agape Worship Center, a rather modern-looking, angular building where the concert would be.

It was dusk now. As we neared the building, I saw three deer browsing on the dry grass out front. They casually moved away as we approached.

Inside, a small lobby area contained a couple of tables, a handful of folding chairs, and a ticket-taker stationed by the door to the main room. We handed over our tickets and went in, shedding our coats.

The worship center was more of a modest auditorium than a church. A single microphone stood in the center of the stage, with a small table beside it. Toward the back of the stage were a drum set and an electric keyboard on a stand. Despite our being a little early, the hall was already filling up, but we found good seats in the sixth row. A few minutes later, the lights dimmed and a tall man in native dress, his long, dark hair flowing over his shoulders, beads jangling a little and buckskin fringe swaying from his sleeves and leggings, walked out to the microphone. He carried several flutes, a rattle, and a small drum, which he placed on the table.

The chatter in the room subsided gradually as the man stood gazing out at us. Seconds seemed to tick slowly by. I found myself wishing the last few whisperers would shut up; couldn't they tell they were delaying the music?

When the hall was finally quiet, the man opened his mouth and sang. The words meant nothing to me—they'd be Tiwa, the language of Taos Pueblo—but the emotion came through loud and clear. Passion, love, despair and hope, all jumbled together into a song that was a cry, an invocation, a call.

I'd heard Bernardo Milagro's music before, but I'd never seen him perform live. He was amazing. He picked up a flute, and made it sing as he had sung, with deep emotion and power. He played his drum and chanted songs that seemed to rise straight up out of the earth, waking distant memories of childhood visits to pueblo dances at Tesuque, Santa Clara, and San Ildefonso. He danced to the heartbeat of the rattle, chanting. He spoke in the sing-song storyteller's voice, of his home, his legends, his family. He sang in Tiwa, English, and Spanish, and for the first hour he did all this alone. When he took a break, leaving the stage with the promise of returning shortly, the audience breathed a collective sigh and then burst into applause.

I looked at Tony.

"Wow," he said.

"Yeah."

We got up to stretch our legs. A handful of kids in scout uniforms were now selling cupcakes at one of the tables in the lobby. Another table held Milagro's CDs and books, as well as two ornate flutes and a some beaded jewelry, made by Milagro according to a small sign. A young Pueblo woman seated behind this table, dressed elegantly in black, watched us calmly as I looked through the CDs. There were no prices on anything, but I didn't care. At least one of these CDs was coming home with me.

I scanned the song listings for titles that sounded familiar. There was no printed program for the night's music, so I had to guess. A song called "Deer Dance" rang a bell, so I held out the CD toward the woman.

"How much is this one?" I asked.

"They're all twenty dollars," she replied.

A bit steep, but the money was going to a deserving artist, and I'd much rather buy directly from Milagro than through a store or online seller, which would take a hefty cut of the proceeds. I fished a twenty out of my purse.

"Would you like him to sign it?" asked the woman.

"That would be great!"

"Bring it back here after," she said, lifting her chin.

"Thanks!"

Clutching my prize, I stepped back to make room for other customers. Tony dutifully admired the CD, and we talked about the first half of the show. He'd been impressed with the variety of Milagro's music, from contemporary—almost jazzy—to what Tony called "woo-woo," to what I thought sounded like authentic traditional Pueblo songs.

The lobby was now fairly crowded. I scanned the faces, looking for Lisette, but didn't see her. I hoped the pastels were giving her an outlet for her feelings.

"Let's go out and get some air," Tony suggested.

"OK."

The night air bit cold and sharp, reminding us that it was winter, and that we were more than a mile above sea level. I hastily put on my coat. Tony stepped forward, listening to the night. In the light of a high-riding quarter moon, he looked like a warrior: smelling the wind, listening for the footfall of hunter or prey. Then he remembered me, led me a few steps away from the door, stepped behind me, and wrapped his arms around me. I leaned into him, sighing, looking up at a sky absolutely powdered with stars. Despite the moon, I could still see the cloudy path of the Milky Way sweeping across the heavens.

This was lovely. This was why we had come here. The tearoom and Tony's job seemed far away.

The moon stood still as a scrap of cloud slid across it, shades of silver-gray and white against the velvet black night. The colors reminded me of O'Keeffe's *Black Place III.* Just as my neck was beginning to complain from my staring at the sky, Tony spoke.

"They're blinking the lobby lights. Time to go in."

Sorry as I was to leave the glory of the night sky, it was good to return to the warmth and light of the auditorium. We hurried back to our seats as the lights began to dim.

For the second half, Milagro was joined by a drummer and a pianist, both young men—possibly also Puebloans judging by their coloring—dressed in black shirts and pants. The music became more complex and varied, from rock to classical to improvisational, ranging far and yet always returning to the yearning, wild strains of the flute, the sing-song shapes of traditional melodies. I loved every minute, and was sad when it ended. Milagro did one encore—in English—a plea and a prayer that we could all come together to heal the world of pain and grief. In that moment, I would have followed him anywhere.

The audience rose to their feet, applauding. I clapped until my hands hurt. After acknowledging the drummer and the pianist, Milagro bowed one final time, hands clasped, and left the stage.

The lights came up, and the audience filed out reluctantly, talking in hushed voices about the music, unwilling to break the mood. This didn't last long. By the time we reached the lobby, it was normal chatter again. Saving the world was forgotten; people wanted coffee and to know how the game had turned out.

A line had formed at the table where Milagro's CDs were on sale. Most of the recordings were gone, and several of the books, and a lot of the jewelry. One gorgeous flute remained, made of hand-shaped and polished wood, adorned with beadwork and a bear fetish carved from obsidian. I didn't dare speculate on its price. Holding my CD, I stood to one side and hoped that the young woman selling the wares would remember her offer of the artist's autograph. I didn't hear her making the same offer to the other customers, though a couple of other people were hanging around like me.

"Want to get some coffee?" Tony asked.

"OK—but I'd like to get this signed," I murmured, lifting my CD.

Tony nodded, shoving his hands in his pockets. We waited while the crowd dwindled. Tony went into people-watching mode. The young Pueblo woman sold the last of the CDs. For something to do, I looked at the remaining books. One was a memoir, and the other was a book of poetry. I leafed through it, and recognized some of the poems as lyrics of songs that Milagro had sung that night.

"I'd like to buy this," I said when the woman was free.

She nodded, and took my cash. I hoped I would have enough left to get me through Sunday; I hadn't planned on buying books and music.

Finally, when only myself and a couple of other hangers-on remained, all of us holding CDs, Milagro emerged from the auditorium. He had changed out of his buckskins into a simple white cotton shirt and jeans, hair still flowing loose. Up close, his eyes were gentle, with fine lines worn by sun and smiles. I realized he was older than I'd thought, maybe forty or fifty—or sixty. Hard to tell. He looked tired, in the satisfied way one felt after a good day's (or night's) work.

He hugged the young woman who'd sold his music, and I noticed a family resemblance. His daughter?

Then he turned to us, holding out his hands to each of us in turn, greeting us like friends, listening kindly to jumbled words of praise. He must have heard it all before. He was a consummate musician, and more—he had made magic in that hall, that night.

When my turn came, he smiled as he signed my CD and then my book, asking my name in a soft voice. His gaze strayed to Tony and held for a second, then he gave a nod and returned his attention to me.

"I'd like to play this at my wedding," I said on impulse, indicating the CD.

Milagro gave me an amused smile, then glanced at Tony again. "Getting married soon?"

"Fall," Tony said.

Milagro looked from one to the other of us. "Sure," he said. "'Dragonfly Song' is a good one." He turned to his daughter and said something in Tiwa. She shook her head. Milagro glanced at the table, then reached over and picked up a small necklace of buckskin and beads. He put it in my hands, clasped them for a moment, then reached over to Tony and brought his hand into the clasp.

"Little wedding present," he said, gently shaking our joined hands. "Blessing."

"Thank you," I said, feeling breathless. "I—you honor us."

He smiled, then released our hands and turned to the next customer.

I stepped back, watching, not wanting to leave. Tony took my elbow and nudged me toward the door. I let him escort me out, clutching the gift and the book and the music. A magical night.

The cold air struck me like a slap, startling me out of my dreamy daze. We hurried back to our room as quickly as we dared in the dark. Tony took out his phone and used it for a flashlight, shining its light on the path ahead of our feet.

Our room was dark, quiet, and a bit cool. Shivering, I put my treasures on the bed and grabbed my sweater out of the closet, pulling it on.

"Still want coffee?" I asked, trying to keep my teeth from chattering.

"You can make tea, right?" Tony said.

"Uh-huh."

"Then let's stay here."

Grateful, I bustled to put on the kettle. I hadn't brought anything herbal, which I now regretted, but if black tea kept me awake, oh well. I needed the warmth. I was glad that I'd bought the second mug, and also that I had taken the time earlier to fetch a bucket of ice to keep the leftover milk cold. I made our tea strong and sweet, with the milk for comfort. We sat huddled together on the bed as we drank it.

"That was amazing," Tony said.

"Uh-huh."

"What was it he gave you?"

"Us," I said, reaching behind me for the necklace. "He gave it to us."

Our first shared possession. I hadn't looked at it closely. Now, with better light, I saw that it was a dragonfly, its long body a slender, clear crystal, probably quartz. The wings were made of tiny iridescent beads, the eyes two larger black beads, maybe obsidian. It hung from a strip of butter-soft leather, reinforced with more beads.

I held it out to Tony. He took it carefully, turning it over in his hands. "That's beautiful work."

I nodded. He looked at me, then slipped the necklace over my head. The dragonfly settled over my heart. We shared a long look, then Tony kissed me. A loving kiss. A sweet, gentle kiss.

Magical night.

The morning light was softer than it had been the previous day, seeping gradually into the room. I was aware of it for a while before I came fully awake. Music ran through my head—a haunting chanting accompanied by rattle and drum. My body wanted to rise and stretch, but the bed was warm and the air on my face was cool. Tony a furnace beside me. I buried my chilled nose in his shoulder and squeezed my eyes shut.

Too late. He was awake, and with a sleepy groan he sat up, letting cold air into the bed.

"Time's breakfast end?" he mumbled.

"Eight-thirty," I said.

"Mm." He shuffled off to the bathroom.

I reached for my phone to check the time. Almost eight. Time to rise. We needed to be dressed, fed, and ready to ride by ten.

The music was fading away, shredding into ghost-like wisps. It had run through my dreams, I remembered, but I couldn't remember what the dreams were about.

I got out of bed and bumped up the thermostat, then got out my clothes for the day. Might as well dress in the riding clothes—except for the boots. Sneakers were more comfortable for walking around.

Outside, the sky was overcast, and the air distinctly cool. I went back for my coat, then matched Tony's stride as we headed for the dining hall.

We made it to breakfast with ten minutes to spare. Tony loaded a plate with biscuits and gravy. I opted for eggs and hash browns with a side of fruit.

The hall was fairly full, but more quiet than usual. The murmur of voices was not augmented by the loud tones of Wesley Roan. I looked around and spotted Lisette and Jeremy seated near the fireplace. No Wesley.

Tony led me to the nearest open table. I hurried through my breakfast, watching for a chance to catch Lisette near the drinks, but she didn't get up from her table until she was ready to leave. She and her son turned in their dishes and went out the far door. If she ever glanced my way, I couldn't tell, because she'd kept her sunglasses on.

The breakfast line had closed down. Feeling chilly, I went back for seconds on coffee, and sat nursing it while Tony finished devouring his heap of biscuits. A few others lingered over their food and coffee.

I took out my map to remind myself of how to get to the stables. There were a bunch of buildings between the dining hall and the corrals, but it looked like we could cut through the welcome center and shorten the walk.

We went back to our room to change into boots and collect hats for the ride. I had brought heavy socks, which I hoped would be enough to protect my heels from blisters on the walk. I seldom wore the boots, so they were still rather stiff.

I filled my water bottle. Dad had drummed it into me to always carry water in the desert, even on a short hike. Hat and coat, sunglasses in case the cloud cover blew off, and I was ready.

Tony demanded a long kiss before opening the door. Still tingling, I walked with him to the welcome center. The snack bar was again closed, with a sign instructing anyone who wanted to buy a drink or one of the box lunches on display (sandwich and chips) to go to the trading post.

"You know what? I'm going to hit the restroom," Tony said.

"OK. I'll wait here."

The snack bar had three empty wrought-iron café tables, with chairs. I admired the movie posters on the walls, all from projects I thought were filmed at least partly in New Mexico, maybe here at the ranch. The widescreen TV was not playing its video at the moment. Next to it, I noticed a computer and printer on a small desk. The equivalent of a hotel's business center, I realized.

Maybe I could use the computer to look up the meaning of Ghost Ranch's name. I went over to it and poked the keyboard. It woke up, so I sat in the chair and brought up a web browser. A search yielded the Ghost Ranch website, but I was more interested in the Wikipedia entry. What it told me was illuminating.

The Archuleta brothers, those cattle-rustlers of yore, were the first people who had lived on the land, in the early twentieth century. They hid their stolen animals up a box canyon, leading the cattle through meandering streams so there'd be no sign of their passing. As if this wasn't theatrical enough, rumors told of the occasional disappearance of a guest of the Archuletas. They had actually buried gold on the ranch, the spoils of their crimes. They argued over it, and one brother killed the other, then held his brother's wife and daughter hostage until they told him where the gold was hidden. The women escaped, and men from the community formed a posse, caught the remaining Archuleta brother, and hanged him from a cottonwood on the ranch—one that was still standing, next to one of the casitas.

Next to *my* casita, I realized. The Ghost House.

I swallowed, wondering which of the two cottonwoods was the hanging tree. Not that it mattered.

The entry added that some people claimed to have heard the voices of a man and woman arguing at night beneath the tree. This echoed what the woman who had checked us in had told me.

Tony joined me. "Bored?" he asked.

I closed the browser and stood. "No. I wanted to know why

our casita is called the Ghost House."

"Did you find out?"

"Yes."

I told him the story as we went out the back door and down a set of rough, earthen steps, then up a long slope toward the stables, passing another block of dormitory lodgings. It sounded even more lurid as I recounted it.

"Huh," was Tony's only remark.

Yeah.

I was glad I had not just heard that story as I was trying to go to sleep on our first night here. It lent a dark edge to the rather wholesome image of Ghost Ranch. I couldn't decide if I was glad I now knew the history. I decided to forget about it and admire the scenery. That was what I had come for, after all: O'Keeffe's landscapes.

This morning, the colors of the cliffs were muted by the overcast sky; a different palette, equally varied but softer, more pastel. Shadows in shades of gray instead of black. The same view, yet different. No wonder O'Keeffe had been fascinated with this area.

By the time we reached the stables, I had unzipped my coat and stuffed my scarf in a pocket. Several cars were parked near the corral, and a number of horses under saddle were tied around the inside of the fence, looking bored.

Voices led us to the barn, where the red-headed cowboy was chatting with half a dozen guests, including Lisette and Jeremy. He paused to greet us, his gaze passing over me with a flicker. No leer today, possibly because of Tony's presence.

"I'm Ted," he said, very politely. "You all ridden before?"

"Yeah," Tony said, as I said, "Yes."

"I need a deputy trail boss to bring up the rear. My partner's out sick this morning."

Tony didn't quite roll his eyes. "Sure," he said.

"You ridden a lot?" Ted asked.

"Used to work my uncle's ranch."

"OK, great. I just need you to sign this waiver—you, too, ma'am," he added, handing each of us a clipboard with pen attached on a string.

While we filled out the paperwork, Ted continued chatting up the others. I recognized some of them from the studio tour: the three middle-aged ladies and the silent, short-haired woman. Most had some experience on horseback, but not a lot. From the sound of it, even my summer-camp background put me in the "pro" category. Tony and I were the only New Mexicans in the group.

I handed Ted my clipboard, then looked toward Lisette. She still wore a tailored, quilted jacket, dark glasses, and a headwrap that reminded me of a hijab. I couldn't tell if I actually caught her eye, but I gave her a friendly nod. She nodded back, then turned away, saying something to Jeremy. He rolled his eyes—with the eloquence only a child could express—and stuffed his phone and earbuds into the pocket of his hoodie.

Ted lined us up along an empty section of fence, then took us one at a time to make the acquaintance of our mounts, listen to a story about each one, and finally achieve the saddle with the aid of a mounting block—something my camp friends would have scoffed at. The process was laborious, so while the second guest was being mounted I turned to Lisette.

"Everything OK?"

She pursed her lips, and her head moved slightly toward her son. "There was a discussion last night."

Jeremy flashed an indignant look at her. "It was a *fight.* You had a fight. Why don't you just say it?"

"That's enough," Lisette said, in a cold voice I hadn't heard from her before.

Jeremy subsided.

"I'm so sorry," I said, feeling my cheeks grow hot. "I didn't mean to pry."

Lisette dismissed this with a tiny shake of her head. "It's nothing new. Unfortunately."

Ted approached, holding a sheet of paper which he glanced at. "Your third gonna join us?" he asked Lisette.

"Apparently not."

"All right, then. Let's get you two in the saddle. You a boss rider, son?" He said to Jeremy.

Jeremy's expression showed his contempt for this cajolery. If Ted noticed, he hid it well. He led the boy over to a pinto and gave him the capsule lesson.

Tony had strolled a few steps away. I doubted he'd missed a word, but he could be discreet. I looked at Lisette with a rueful smile.

"Maybe your husband just didn't want to ride."

"I know he didn't. That's not the issue. We did argue last night, and he stormed out."

"He left?"

"He does it now and then. He'll be back."

She didn't sound as if she looked forward to this. I felt such pity for her, but I sensed she didn't want it.

I wondered if small talk about O'Keeffe and pastels and drawing would be any comfort, but before I could try it, Ted returned and took Lisette over to a palomino. The horse tossed its head restlessly. Ted laid a hand on its neck, and a moment later Lisette did the same.

Four horses remained at the fence. The mounted riders were standing in line where Ted had placed them. Most looked afraid to move. As I watched, Ted led Lisette's horse into the line behind her son.

It was my turn. My mount was an undistinguished liver chestnut. Not even a star or a sock; just a brown, brown horse. Ted introduced him as "Chui" and gave me more than I wanted to know of his life's story, then supervised my mounting with the block, ready to correct any gross errors—an opportunity I did not give him.

He led Chui into line behind Lisette's mount, then returned to Tony. I could hear them chatting, though I couldn't see them without craning around in the saddle. Ted apparently took Tony at his word; he didn't bother with the mounting block. Tony mounted at the fence and joined the string behind me.

The last two horses were a roan and a gigantic bay. Ted turned the bay out into an adjacent corral, still saddled but without its bridle, and returned to mount the roan. The bay meandered over to a manger and began lipping at the hay.

"All right! Let's get a move on," Ted yelled, riding to the front of the string. He called out cheerful reminders to keep the line closed up, hold the reins loosely, and lean a little forward. The horses plodded sleepily after him. They knew the drill, well enough to be bored by it. A couple of them flicked envious ears toward the big bay enjoying his early snack.

The first five minutes were spent negotiating a route away from the ranch buildings. We soon turned onto a trail worn deep into the ground, evidence of the long history of this activity. A small hope that Ted would open up to a trot once we were away from the buildings faded. We continued across a mesa at a snail's pace. Deadly dull. I kept an eye on Lisette, watching for any nervousness. Horses could smell uncertainty, and a cranky horse would take advantage of it to divest itself of its rider. Fortunately, Lisette's confidence had apparently earned her mount's respect.

Now and then Ted shouted something over his shoulder. Unfortunately, I was too far back to understand him. This boded ill for my learning anything about O'Keeffe on the ride. I felt sorry for Tony, who was even farther from the narration, but then, he wasn't too interested in what Ted had to say. He was just happy to be in the saddle.

The sky remained pearly gray. The air was still, which was good, because the horse's hooves were raising plenty of dust. The lightest breeze would make it worse.

You are here to have fun, I reminded myself.

Seeking evidence of fun, I gazed around at the scenery. We were headed roughly northwest, skirting the cliffs at a good viewing distance, across a mostly barren, slightly hilly landscape. Scrub sage and an occasional juniper or piñon were the largest plants in view. The trail we followed was a good half inch deep in dust from the twice-daily passing of horses. Our mounts could have traversed it in their sleep. Perhaps they were.

As we crested a hill, Ted halted us and called our attention to the cliffs. Still too far to catch everything he said, I caught enough to know that he wasn't making any startling revelations. "Sandstone" and "vista" were the only words I was sure of. Chimney Rock was visible to our right. I gazed at the cliffs, trying to recall an O'Keeffe painting that featured this particular view.

While in residence at the ranch, she had done many, many paintings of what she referred to as her back yard, or her front yard, depending which way you were looking. Front yard, I decided. The back yard was to the south, where the distinctive flat-topped hump of *Pedernal* rose above the plateau.

The string moved forward again, descending a short, steep slope into an arroyo. I leaned back as I had learned to do on many a trail ride, to help the horse balance as it descended. A startled yelp from the front of the line drew my attention; Ted had already moved to aid a less experienced rider, his hand hovering above her mount's reins while she recovered her balance on her skittering horse. It had descended the last few steps rather quickly, I deduced.

Lisette and Jeremy were doing fine. Their position in the middle of the string kept them safe; their horses didn't have much opportunity to vary from the routine. A glimpse I caught of Jeremy's face revealed his disgust with this situation. Ah, well. Maybe once we were heading back toward the stables, he'd get a chance to trot a bit. The horses would certainly be willing, in that direction.

Chui let out a bored huff as we halted behind Lisette's palomino. Ted was still calming the startled rider up ahead, talking in soothing tones, touching the horse and encouraging her to do the same. I patted Chui's neck.

"Just think about the hay that's waiting for you when we get back," I suggested. Chui sidled and craned his head around to give me a sidelong glance. "Yes, but I'm sure there's more in the barn," I reminded him.

Behind me, Tony snorted softly. I thought I heard a chuckle from Lisette. Smiling, I gathered up my reins as the string moved forward once more.

Ted stopped a couple more times, but mostly just shouted his descriptions over his shoulder. I caught random words: "academy," "tree," "skull," "New York." They evoked chapters in the biography; I was content to deduce my own narrative based on these recollections. I was thankful for the book, which I planned to continue reading.

We reached a small, adobe homestead protected by a teetery rail fence and large, unfriendly signs that said "KEEP OUT." I recognized it as O'Keeffe's ranch house, her first home at Ghost Ranch (not counting the casitas she had rented early on). She'd bought the house from the ranch's owner, and had done many famous paintings here. Ted shouted a bit of history at us as we circled past it, and told us that it was not open to the public.

An ancient, dilapidated ladder made of wooden poles still rested against the house in the courtyard. I knew from the biography that O'Keeffe had climbed onto the roof every evening to watch the sunset. Glancing westward, I admired the distant mountains, picturing the clouded sky lit with raspberry and orange.

We rode on toward that future sunset, following the trail across flats and through arroyos. Ted continued to narrate. I hoped the people at the front of the string were enjoying it; I had long since given up. The tour was not all I had hoped for, though the scenery was undeniably beautiful. New Mexico at its best.

On a flat stretch, I took a sip from my water bottle. I was beginning to get hungry. I wished I'd brought some nuts or something in addition to the water. The tour was ninety minutes long, and we were not quite halfway through.

We made a final stop to admire the red and yellow *Piedra Lumbre* cliffs—highly recognizable from O'Keeffe's work. I actually heard most of what Ted said on this occasion. I didn't learn anything I hadn't already known, but it was a nice summing up of the landscape and O'Keeffe's time in the ranch house. I found myself comparing this area to the sweeping views and the beautiful studio up in Abiquiu that we had toured the previous day. More rustic here, and her life had been austere. Once she moved to Abiquiu, comfort had become a priority, though she remained aloof from the community.

Tony sidled his horse up beside mine. "You're not hearing much of the tour guide, are you?"

"No, but I read the book. I'm fine. Are you bored?"

"Nah. It's good to be out in the fresh air. Good to be on horseback. I didn't realize how much I missed it." He gave his mount a pat on the neck. The horse nickered softly; they'd made friends. Tony had a way with horses, I realized. I'd never seen him interacting with an animal before, but he was clearly a natural. I wondered if he'd ever had pets, but before I could ask, Ted started the string moving again.

The trail made a wide swing northward and then back toward the south, so we didn't have to double back. As we went around the turn, we came within a few yards of a barbed wire fence that had seen better days. Between two haphazard log fenceposts, the top wire sagged under the weight of a large, hand-painted sign that said "PRIVATE PROPERTY – Trespassers will be PROSECUTED to the full extent of the LAW!" It continued in that vein, the words getting smaller the farther down the sign they went. I lost interest.

Ted led us along the dry bottom of an arroyo that snaked between low hills, giving tantalizing glimpses of the cliffs from different angles. Deciduous trees—cottonwoods and the ever-present invader, Siberian elm—grew in and alongside the arroyo, their branches bare and gray this time of year. I admired them, picturing them in full leaf in summer green, autumn gold.

Abruptly, the trail went up the side of the arroyo, climbing fifteen feet or so in a couple of switchbacks. I took a last look along the arroyo at the trees—and saw something out of place.

Instinctively I pulled on my reins as I gave a little gasp. Chui, finally headed back toward the barn, protested, but obeyed.

"What is it?" Tony asked, reining in beside me.

Unable to speak, I pointed.

Had we kept riding in the arroyo, we would all have seen it. At a bend a short distance along stood a tall cottonwood, its branches hanging over the dry waterway. One of them hung lower than the others.

It was pulled down by the weight of a man's body, twisting gently in the breeze at the end of a rope.

7

I COULDN'T LOOK AWAY, because I wondered...suspected...feared... that the body was Wesley Roan.

Black head to toe: black clothing, black shoes, dark head. I was too far away to be sure, but the pit of my stomach was telling me the worst was true.

"Stay here," Tony told me, and he was gone, up the steep switchbacks, his horse breaking into a run as he reached the top and passed Lisette. I listened to the hoofbeats receding and tried to catch my breath.

Lisette's horse jibbed, objecting to Tony's passage. Should I go to help her? But she got the horse under control and it continued walking, following the string, disappearing from view.

I was alone in the arroyo. Alone with the body.

Tony had told me to stay. Why? For my safety? Or to keep an eye on the body?

As a cop, his instinct would be to protect the evidence of a crime. That must be it; I was standing witness until he could return.

I swallowed, not much liking this duty. Chui took a step toward the path up the arroyo, and I halted him again. He subsided, lowering his head and shaking it as he blew, an expression of disgust.

My mouth was dry. I sipped from my water bottle, then secured it, all the while paying attention to what Chui was doing, because I knew that if I got distracted, he'd take advantage.

I didn't want to think about Wesley Roan, about what had

happened to him, and why. A hate crime, obviously. The age-old symbolism of a hanging tree. It made me feel sick.

I couldn't help thinking of the Archuleta brothers. Voices under the cottonwood, restless ghosts walking the ranch. Campfire tales, but based in truth from a hundred years ago, when the West had been wilder.

Hoofbeats tickled my hearing in the distance. They got louder. More than one horse. In a swirl of dust, Tony returned with Ted. They descended the trail and joined me.

"Aw, hell," said Ted, looking toward the cottonwood and its burden. He took out a hand-held radio.

Why not a phone? I pulled my cell out of my pocket and got the answer. No bars.

No cell towers out here, in O'Keeffe's empty wilds.

Ted connected with someone and swiftly exchanged details. I looked at Tony.

"Do you have to call this in?" I asked softly.

"I'll talk to County, but the Ranch people need to report it."

I looked down, feeling sad at what I knew lay ahead. Not only would Tony have to talk to the county sheriffs, so would I.

Staring at the ground beneath my horse's hooves, I noticed tire tracks in the dust, partly obscured by hoofprints. Not unusual; arroyos were a common place for off-roading.

"Where are the others?" I asked.

"Waiting on the mesa," Tony said.

"Should I go join them?"

He looked toward the tree, then at me. Concern showed in the tightness of his facial muscles. "Yeah, you don't need to stay. Don't say anything to them."

"I know."

I gathered my reins and nudged Chui toward the side of the arroyo. That was all it took; I had to rein him in to keep him from running up the trail. At the top I saw the string stopped a little way ahead. Obedient, the riders had stayed where they were, facing the way home. Their horses sidled and fretted. I gave Chui enough rein that he trotted the short distance to the string.

Lisette turned her head as I approached. I guided Chui off the track and halted beside her.

"What is it?" she asked.

The question I'd been dreading.

"I'm not sure," was all I could come up with. "There's a problem," I added lamely.

Lisette frowned. "What problem?"

A surge of sorrow overcame me. If my suspicions were right, Lisette and her son were about to be embroiled in one of the worst things that could happen to a family. At the same time, I knew that Tony would want me to watch how she reacted when she learned about it. I was suddenly glad that I was prohibited from telling her.

Jeremy craned around in the saddle to look at us. "What's going on, Mom?"

I heard a horse climbing the bank behind me. I turned Chui sideways, so I could see Ted as he reached the top of the arroyo. He trotted toward us, glanced at me, then at Lisette.

"Sorry for the delay," he said. "We'll head back now."

He rode on to the head of the string, past the sidling horses. A moment later we started forward.

I fell in behind Lisette, glad that it was inconvenient to talk as we rode single file. Lisette needed to concentrate on riding, and I needed time to figure out what to say to her once she learned what had happened.

What I *suspected* had happened. But my gut told me I knew.

Someone had hanged Wesley Roan.

Why?

Good lord, why not? From what I'd seen, he was a complete jerk, rude to everyone he met, full of himself and uninterested in anyone else. Cruel to his family, which I found hard to forgive. Yet I knew that they'd suffer from his loss.

Who could have killed Wesley? I couldn't imagine any individual doing it.

A posse.

Had Wesley Roan made himself so obnoxious that a group of men had joined forces to hang him? Like the last Archuleta brother?

"Whoa, there!"

I looked up toward the head of the string, where Ted was collecting a wayward horse and getting it back into line. It had started off cross country, maybe in a more direct line toward the barn, and its rider—the short-haired woman—was cussing up a storm.

All the horses were edgy. They knew something was wrong.

With an effort, I forced myself to stop thinking about the tree and the arroyo behind us. I pictured the dining hall, the lunch line. Something delicious awaited us there, I told myself.

My tongue was stuck to the roof of my mouth, and the thought of food was not enticing.

It seemed to take forever to get back to the barn. There were no more stops, no more shouted narrations from Ted about O'Keeffe and her work, and why the hell did any of that matter anyway? A man was dead. Hanged from a tree not a mile behind us. We were *all* about to have a terrible time.

But it would be worst for the Roans, Lisette and Jeremy. More alone than ever now, in a place that was alien to them, and maybe —probably—felt unwelcoming. I made up my mind to try to help them, to stand by them as much as I could.

But what if—?

What if's didn't matter, I told myself. They were a family suddenly fractured. They would need support. Deciding whether they'd been involved in Wesley's death wasn't my job. I'd made a tenuous connection with Lisette, and it was probable that I was the only semblance of a friend she had at this place and time.

I wondered what Tony was doing. Standing guard over the body, no doubt, until the sheriffs arrived. Heaven knew when I'd see him.

When we finally got back to the barn, everyone's mood was frayed, and the sight of an SUV with a badge and "Rio Arriba County Sheriff" painted on the side was no help. Two men sat inside it, hunched down behind their shades.

Ted helped the riders dismount, one by one. I slid from the saddle on my own and led Chui to the fence where I'd met him. I looped the reins loosely over the rail, gave the horse a farewell pat, and got out of the way.

A pickup with the Ghost Ranch logo pulled up beside the SUV. A tall man I didn't recognize, wearing a sheepskin coat and a battered cowboy hat, got out and went to talk to the sheriffs. After a minute, he returned to the truck, backed out, and drove up road that went northward. The SUV followed.

That must be the road that the van tour went on. We'd seen it, off and on, as we rode. Just a dirt road that went more or less the same direction as the horse trail, but with less meandering. It passed near O'Keeffe's ranch house, I was certain. I didn't remember if it continued beyond.

All the riders were down now, saying thank you and goodbye to Ted, who looked worried and distracted behind the automatic smile. He gave me a puzzled frown, glanced toward Chui, then fetched him and led him to the back corral. The big bay was there, still saddled, standing by the fence and watching the proceedings with a bored expression.

Lisette walked up to me, with Jeremy following. "What was all that about?" she asked. "Your boyfriend stayed behind."

"My fiancé. Yes." I drew a deep breath. "He's a detective. I'm afraid there was—evidence of a crime."

Lisette's frown deepened. "You saw something?"

I swallowed, nodded.

"What?"

"I—I'm sorry. I shouldn't say."

I couldn't see Lisette's eyes through her shades, but her mouth dropped open a little.

"I'm going to walk down to the snack bar," I said. "I could use some coffee. Want to come along?"

"Our car is here," Lisette said. "Let me give you a lift."

I hesitated just for a second, but my feet were hurting from the boots, and I caved. "Thanks," I said, mustering a smile.

Lisette led the way toward a big, white Cadillac SUV. Jeremy fell in behind me. He already had his earbuds in, though he gave me one suspicious look.

We rode in silence. Lisette was occupied with steering the Cadillac down the rough road to the welcome center, Jeremy was engrossed in his phone, and I was at a loss for words. It was like watching a tornado approach and not knowing where to hide.

I checked my phone, looking for a text from Tony. Nothing, of course. I sent him a text that I was with the Roans.

The snack bar was, again, closed. The dining hall would be open for lunch in less than half an hour. Jeremy wandered into the trading post, but I didn't feel like junk food and cold drinks. I looked at Lisette.

"Want to come to my room for some tea?"

She nodded, and summoned Jeremy, who grumbled slightly but returned with us to the car. I directed Lisette to park next to my Camry, and got out. The sky was still overcast; if anything, it was a little darker. I looked in vain for a bright spot where the sun might break through.

I unlocked the door and invited the Roans into the Room of Many Chairs. Jeremy made himself at home in a chair by the east window, never looking up from his phone. I put the kettle on and puttered with tea leaves and teapot. Lisette sank into the same chair where she'd sat before.

"Were you able to hear the narration about O'Keeffe?" I asked. "I couldn't hear a thing."

"I caught most of it," Lisette said.

I bit back a question about whether she enjoyed the tour. She plainly wasn't enjoying anything at the moment, and it was about to get worse.

Trying to find a happier subject, I asked, "Did you make some drawings yesterday?"

She nodded. A faint smile touched her lips, then faded. "I spent a couple of hours working on a landscape. I'm pretty rusty, but it felt good."

"I'd love to see it," I said.

Lisette's face closed down again. "Wesley tore it up."

"No!" I blurted.

"He came back to the room in a mood. He was looking for a fight, and he made one."

"I'm so sorry," was all I could say.

Lisette shrugged. "That's my life." She glanced at Jeremy, who was paying no attention to us. "I spend a lot of time picking up the pieces."

"Do you want to talk about it?"

Another shrug. "I'll go over it all with my therapist when we get home. That's what I pay her for. You shouldn't have to listen to it."

The kettle began to boil. I made tea, wondering all the while how I could help Lisette. I brought the souvenir cup to her.

"I'm out of milk, I'm afraid. Do you want some sugar?"

She shook her head. "This is fine. Thank you."

I glanced at Jeremy. "Would Jeremy like some?"

"No, he's not a tea drinker. He'll be all right until lunch."

I poured tea for myself in the second mug and took my seat, sipping it. Trying to give Lisette some space, I avoided looking at her, though it wasn't easy. She sat still, only moving to lift the mug and drink now and then. She'd kept the shades on. Hiding behind them. My heart went out to her.

Would she be relieved to know Wesley was dead, I wondered?

Terrible thought, but some small part of her probably would, I reflected. Only one aspect of a complicated reaction, no doubt. Had she ever loved her husband? From what little she'd told me, it sounded like what would once have been called a marriage of convenience.

I couldn't imagine making such a bargain. Trading physical intimacy for financial security, or for social advantage.

My privilege, again. I was blessed with security; I didn't have to make such hard choices. Even in this modern age, others were not so fortunate.

The buzz of a text arriving on my phone startled all of us. I had plugged it in; I jumped up to silence it. The text was from Tony.

> Where are you?

> At our casita. The Roans
> are here. I made tea.

> Keep them there. I'll be
> right over.

"It's Tony," I said. "My fiancé. He's on his way." I glanced at the time on my phone, then set it down and returned to sit on the bed.

Lisette looked in my direction, hands still cradling her mug. She raised it, finished off her tea, and held out the mug to me.

"There's more," I offered, accepting it and gesturing toward the teapot.

Lisette shook her head. "We should go."

"Oh, won't you stay a couple minutes? I'd like to introduce you to Tony. We could all walk over to lunch."

Lisette turned her head toward her son, who was apparently oblivious, engrossed in his phone. "All right," she said. A sigh escaped her and she pulled off her shades to rub at her eyes. It was an unconscious gesture, but it a revealing one.

Bruises are harder to discern on dark skin, I realized. While she had her shades on, I hadn't noticed, but I now saw that she had a shiner on her left eye that extended down onto her elegant cheekbone.

My small, sharp inhalation was involuntary. Lisette looked up at me, realization widening her eyes, and hastily put her shades back on.

"Did your husband do that?" I whispered.

Her face tightened and she gave another, angry sigh, then nodded.

"Dear God!"

The sound of the outer door being unlocked made us both jump. Instinctively I stood, placing myself between the door to the bedroom and Lisette. Tony gave me a questioning look as he came in. I had no answer. He glanced toward Lisette and back to me.

Swallowing, I took one step aside, turning to indicate Lisette with a gesture. Distress made me speak more formally than I'd intended.

"Tony, I'd like you to meet Lisette Roan. Lisette, this is Tony Aragón, my fiancé."

Tony took a step forward, formality descending upon him as well. Cop formality.

"Ma'am."

Lisette sat still. She knew, perhaps from our behavior, that something was quite wrong. Her head turned slightly toward her son, then back to face Tony.

Tony glanced at Jeremy, who was still absorbed in his play world, ignoring us adults. "Mrs. Roan, I'm afraid I have bad news," Tony continued. His voice was gentle, but nothing could soften his message. "Your husband is dead."

Slowly Lisette's lips parted. Her brows drew together. "What happened?" She said in a strangled voice.

I glanced at Tony. He was watching her intently.

"It appears he's been murdered."

Lisette's mouth dropped open, her lower lip trembling slightly, a horrified rictus. I wanted to rush to her and hug her. I stayed still.

"The county sheriffs want to talk with you," Tony said. "They asked me to bring you to the welcome center."

Lisette looked toward her boy. "Jeremy," she said softly, then turned to me. It was a plea, not a summons. She was asking for help.

"They'll want to speak to him, too," Tony added.

"Would you like me to come with you?" I said.

A swallow moved Lisette's throat, and she nodded, then stood and turned to Tony. "May I tell my son?"

Tony stepped back and gestured toward Jeremy, giving silent permission. He would watch, of course—hawk-like, noticing every detail. How had he convinced the local sheriffs to let him break the news? I wondered.

Lisette walked to the second bed and sat beside Jeremy. He glanced at her, still playing, thumbs flying over the screen. She took off her shades, setting them aside, then slowly wrapped her hands around his, until he stopped and looked up at her.

"Jeremy."

Hastily he removed his earbuds. Something in her expression had frightened him.

"This man is a policeman," she said, with the slightest of nods in Tony's direction. "Your father's been killed."

Jeremy's eyes widened and his mouth opened. He looked ready to flee, or to jump up and yell. The flood of confused emotions on his face were too swift to follow, but I thought I saw a flash of anger, and another of—glee? Finally he shoved his phone aside and threw himself into his mother's embrace, burying his face in her shoulder.

I glanced at Tony. His face revealed nothing. Full cop mode.

Jeremy let out a sob. Lisette rocked him back and forth slightly, whispering, "It's OK. It's OK."

We waited while the boy—this insolent, adolescent boy—wept openly. The honesty of his grief, however confused it might be, made my throat tighten. Lisette was silent, the strong mother; or perhaps she had to lock all her feelings away to avoid breaking down as well. I felt so sorry for them both.

After a minute or two, Jeremy's sobbing subsided. Tony gave a quiet cough. "Ma'am, we should go now. Best to get it over with."

Lisette raised her head and shot one glare at Tony, then with one of her short sighs, nodded. She coaxed Jeremy to his feet, keeping an arm around his shoulders. He clung to her like a frightened kitten as they started toward the door.

I collected Jeremy's phone and earbuds, then my own phone. Tony held the door while we filed out. He locked it, and we walked up the path to the welcome center.

I saw Tony type a surreptitious text into his phone. He slid it back into his pocket and stepped out in front of the Roans, walking a little faster, as if to hasten them on. I brought up the rear, keeping an eye on Jeremy in case he stumbled. Occasionally he let out a strangled gulp of a sob.

The sheriffs had taken over one of the offices in the welcome center. They whisked Lisette into it as soon as we arrived, then one of them—taller, younger, and thinner than his partner—returned outside to keep an eye on the rest of us. He looked vaguely familiar, but I wasn't about to stare at him. Rather than stand in the hall, I led Jeremy into the reception room, where there was a bench. Tony followed, keeping us in sight, and the sheriff looked in as well, then returned to the hall, standing where he could see us.

I offered Jeremy his phone and earbuds. He grabbed them, as though frightened that he'd forgotten them. Shoving the buds in his ears, he turned on the phone and ignored me, falling still. I'd expected him to dive into a game, but it looked like he was playing music. His hands were quiet.

And so, we waited. After a while I glanced at my phone, and realized we were not going to get to the dining hall for lunch. I stood and stepped toward Tony.

"I'm going to grab a couple of sandwiches from the snack bar. You want something?"

"Yeah. Anything."

The snack bar had a cooler with pre-made lunches—a sandwich and a bag of chips in a plastic box. Maybe a cookie hiding underneath. They looked boring. I scanned the labels to see what our choices were. They were all labeled "turkey." I went into the trading post and asked to buy three of them, as well as three cans of soda. Returning, I offered Jeremy a box. Mechanically he opened it and started eating, gaze locked on his phone. Tony accepted a sandwich. I opened my box, but couldn't bring myself to eat the sandwich. Instead I opened the potato chips and started nibbling them, one at a time. The sheriff watched us, making no comment.

I had finished the chips, and Tony had eaten his sandwich, when the office door opened and Lisette came out. The sheriff immediately herded Jeremy in. Carrying his half-eaten lunch, the boy shot a frightened glance at his mother before the door closed. Lisette stood still briefly, facing the door, then went to the chair where Jeremy had been sitting. Her shades masked her eyes, but her movements were taut with tension.

"I bought Jeremy a sandwich," I told her. "Would you like half of mine?"

She shook her head.

"Coffee? A soda?"

"No, thank you," she said in a tiny voice.

Her furrowed brow made me suspect she was close to tears. Her long fingers were laced together in her lap. She seemed frozen, in a way: afraid to move, or even think, lest she break down in this public place. I left, giving her space, and threw away the sandwich I couldn't eat.

Jeremy's interview took less time than Lisette's. When he emerged, he ran over to her and threw himself into her arms again. She held him, silently stroking his head.

"Ma'am?"

I looked up and saw the younger sheriff standing over me. He cleared his throat.

"Would you come in, please?"

I knew I'd be interviewed, but hadn't expected it to be immediately. I exchanged a look with Tony, who gave a small nod as if to encourage me.

The office was small. The door was heavy; no sound penetrated. Behind a desk piled with paperwork that was not his own, the senior sheriff sat regarding me. He was Hispanic, maybe forty, about my height and probably twice my weight. His cop stare was probably meant to intimidate, but I was used to Tony and remained unruffled.

"Have a seat," he said.

"Thank you."

I sat in one of the visitor's chairs, a square-framed thing of wood and padded cloth, not unlike some of the chairs in our second room. Utilitarian. Inoffensive. Boring.

The sheriff took down my name and phone number and so forth. His handwriting was slow and painstaking. Finally he looked up at me.

"Tell me how you found the body."

I winced inwardly. I suppose I had found another body. At a

distance, but I was the one who had noticed it. I gave him a concise description of the trail ride, and how I was riding at the back, with Tony behind me, and how I had seen the body hanging from a tree.

"How come you're the only one who saw it?"

"It wasn't in our line of sight. I was looking at the scenery and the trees, and happened to look along the arroyo as the others were climbing the bank."

"Did you know Wesley Roan?"

"No, not at all."

"But you know Mrs. Roan."

"We met this weekend, in the dining hall."

"You just met, and started hanging out together?"

"Women do that," I said.

He stared at me. I stared back.

"She tell you anything about her husband?"

"Yes," I said.

"What?"

"She said he had lots of money, and that he wanted a pretty wife."

The sheriff's eyes narrowed. "What else?"

I thought back. "I think that's all she told me about him."

There were a couple of things she hadn't told me, but had confirmed when I asked. And there were things I had observed about Wesley's behavior. But that's not what the sheriff had asked, and his attitude was patronizing enough that I didn't feel like being helpful. I suspected he wanted to build a case against Lisette, who must of course be a suspect. I felt certain she was innocent, and wasn't about to offer up substantiation for his suspicion.

"What's your impression of Wesley Roan, based on what you saw of him?"

"He was obnoxious."

"To his wife?"

"To everyone, as far as I could tell."

"Did you hear him say anything obnoxious—" He stressed the word slightly, as if sarcastic about my choice of phrase. "—to his wife?"

"I'm not sure I heard him speak to his wife at all. But pretty much everything I heard him say to anyone was rude. The man was a bully."

"A bully? Did he threaten people?"

I thought a moment. "I don't think I ever heard him make a threat. But I wasn't around him much."

"What about arguments?"

"He was in arguments whenever I saw him in the dining hall."

"With anyone in particular?"

"With everyone who'd join in." A memory tickled and I added, "There was a man in a hat with an American Flag on it that he argued especially loudly with. I think it was over football."

"Do you know that man's name?"

"No."

"Can you describe him?"

I did so, pausing now and then to let the sheriff catch up with his notes. He put down the pen and looked at me.

"Did Mr. Roan say anything obnoxious to you?"

"To me? No. He never spoke to me at all."

"What did you think when you saw him hanging from a tree?"

"I didn't know it was him. I was too far away to tell. All I knew was that it looked like a body hanging from a tree, and I was horrified, of course."

He gave me another cop stare. I held his gaze.

"All right," he said finally. He pushed a business card across the desk toward me. "If you think of anything else, call me."

I nodded, picked up the card and glanced at it: SHERIFF ENRICO ROMERO. As I stood and started for the door, he spoke again.

"Are you glad he's dead?"

I turned. "What kind of a question is that?" I asked, rather offended. "A man's been murdered. Why would that make me glad?"

Sheriff Romero shrugged. "You obviously didn't like him."

"That doesn't mean I wanted him dead."

Cop stare, then with a jerk of his head, he invited me to leave. I did so.

I pulled the door shut rather firmly as I stepped out. The younger sheriff, who was approaching, gave me a disconcerted look, then a frown. Having had enough of sheriffs, I put my nose in the air and walked past him to the reception area, where Tony was seated alone, trying not to laugh. His eyes gleamed at me with delight as I sat beside him.

"So, did he break one of Miss Manners's rules?" he asked.

I looked toward the junior sheriff, who had opened the office door. I waited until he went in and closed it before answering.

"He was a bit offensive. He implied that I might be happy about Mr. Roan's death."

Tony looked surprised. "Not too subtle."

"He was not subtle, no."

"Well, he's old school. Traditions are pretty ingrained in Rio Arriba County."

I'd heard that. Not just traditions, but ancient anger could still be found in pockets in northern New Mexico. Growing up, there were rumors, warnings; don't go up to Rio Arriba at night. I remembered a football game when the marching band had accompanied the team to Española, and the girls had been warned not to walk anywhere alone.

"Lisette—Mrs. Roan—she left?" I asked Tony.

"Yeah, her and the kid. He was pretty broken up."

I wished I had thought to give her my phone number. I wanted her to know she had at least one friend here, during this nightmare. She probably had friends at home she could call—certainly her aunt if no one else—but that wasn't the same as being in the room with someone, looking in their eyes. I sighed.

"So..." Tony said. "lunch sucked."

"Yeah. Sorry."

"Want to go find dessert?"

I glanced toward the trading post, with its candy and snacks. "What do you have in mind? We're going to the Abiquiu Inn tonight."

"I hear Bode's has ice cream. They have a little restaurant, too."

"Bode's?"

"That convenience store up the road. Want to check it out?"

I remembered seeing a store on the way up to the O'Keeffe house. "Sure," I said. "Can we go to the room first? These boots are killing my feet."

We walked out and down the path to the Ghost House. The sky had darkened, and a few flakes of snow were drifting around on a chilly breeze. Not ice cream weather, in my opinion, but I sympathized with Tony's desire to get away from Ghost Ranch for a while, and to eat something more interesting than the sandwiches we'd had.

As we walked, I scanned the surroundings, hoping for a glimpse of Lisette. There were not many people out and about. The air was still, as if weighed down by the glowering clouds. I shoved my chilled hands in the pockets of my jacket. When we were skirting the Ghost House's courtyard to get to our room, the house's door opened and the short-haired woman stepped out. She gave us a startled look, then hurried away up the path.

Our bedroom room was blessedly warm when we stepped in. I took off my coat, changed into my walking shoes, put on my sweater, then put the coat back on. Tony didn't bother changing out of his cowboy boots. He must have been more comfortable in them than I ever had been, or perhaps he was still enjoying memories of being a ranch hand. That kind of tedious work was always better as a memory than as a reality.

We went out to my car. The Roans' SUV was still next to it, empty. I had an idea, opened my purse, found a business card, and wrote my cell number on it, with "Please call" beside it. I tucked it in the window of the driver door.

"That's the Roans' car," I said in answer to Tony's inquiring look.

"Ah. You know, you shouldn't talk to them about the murder."

"I don't intend to, but she's alone here, except for her son. I just want to offer some emotional support."

"Fair enough."

We got in my car and I drove gingerly down the dirt road to the highway. The events of the morning had left me feeling rather forlorn, and the weather wasn't helping. Gray skies made the landscape look washed out, desolate. The vibrant colors were muted. Living things were hidden or asleep, mostly. Winter indeed.

Bode's was just a few minutes' drive. Several gas pumps stood outside, but when we went inside I realized it was not just a convenience store. It was much bigger than I had expected, and much better stocked: obviously a hub for the wider, more dispersed community in the Chama River valley. There were an impressive array of wines, huge stacks of cases of beer, racks of T-shirts and other clothing, and a rather intimidating shelf of "outdoor gear" including several varieties of hunting knives.

There was even a decent selection of better-quality teas, albeit in teabags.

Plenty of activity here as well; half a dozen people were shopping, and a hubbub of voices came from the tables by the lunch counter. Tony and I strolled over that way. The menu wasn't long, but had enough variety that if I'd been a long-time guest at Ghost Ranch I would probably have come to Bode's now and then for a change of pace. I spotted espresso drinks on the list and ordered a cappuccino, along with a fresh-baked muffin to share with Tony, who opted for regular coffee. He gallantly picked up the tab, and we tucked ourselves into the modest chairs at a tiny table for two.

"Mm," Tony said, after sampling his coffee. "Better than the cafeteria."

I sipped my cappuccino—very comforting—and sighed. "What a morning."

"Yeah. Gonna be rough when you go back to work."

I blinked. "Why?"

"You're gonna have to tell your people you found another body."

I reached across and whapped his shoulder as he chortled. "It's not funny!"

"Face it, babe. It's a thing."

My shoulders slumped. "I'm a corpse-magnet."

"A *what?*"

"That's what the Bird Woman called me."

He laughed helplessly. "D-damn!"

"It's not funny," I said, struggling not to laugh.

Tony gave up and laughed aloud, squeezing his eyes shut.

"Tony Aragón, stop laughing or I won't share my muffin with you!"

"Hey, I paid for that muffin!"

"Well, it's mine now." To demonstrate possession, I picked it up and peeled off the baking paper wrapper. A whiff of spice reached me, and I tore off a chunk of the soft, moist muffin and ate it. My stomach, which had been hunkered down and uncooperative, grudgingly approved this offering.

Tony managed to control himself, and held out his hand. I divided the muffin and gave him his share. His eyes were still laughing, but at least with his mouth full he couldn't say anything offensive.

"I wonder who killed him," I said quietly.

Tony swallowed. "Not our job."

"I know. I just—I'm amazed at how many possibilities there are. We first saw him yesterday morning, and I can count off half a dozen people he angered since then."

"More than that," Tony said.

"More?"

"You didn't watch the football game."

"Oh. Was he awful?"

"Any time anyone said anything against the Texans, or in favor of the Cowboys, he was ready to pick a fight. If you even cheered for the Cowboys, he'd cuss you or call you a name."

"Did he do that to you?" I asked in a small voice.

"He did it to *everyone*. He took all the fun out of watching the game. That's why I didn't stick around."

I wrapped my hands around my warm cup and sipped. The cappuccino was just the perfect temperature now, so I took a bigger swallow. "Was his son there?"

"Yeah. Kid was trying to watch the game, but he was obviously embarrassed by his dad's behavior."

"Poor Jeremy."

"That kid's gonna have problems," Tony said.

"He's already got problems."

"One less, at least."

I looked up, thinking that rather a cold remark, but Tony's face showed sympathy for the boy's position. And what he'd said was true. I remembered the flash of glee, however short, that I had glimpsed on Jeremy's face when his mother told him the bad news.

What a mess.

I glanced at my phone. No calls or texts. It was just after one o'clock, and we had an empty afternoon. We'd had a half-conceived plan of hiking again, or driving over to look at the White Place, but the weather was off-putting. Indoor activities would be preferable.

"Maybe we could visit the museum," I mused aloud.

"Dinosaur bones?"

I shrugged. "It's something to do."

"Rather catch a movie."

"We'd have to drive to Española."

"They have some DVDs in the cantina, where we watched the game."

"Oh. But isn't there another game on? I mean, wouldn't people be watching something already?"

"Maybe. Worth looking, though."

I conceded this, though I wasn't terribly enthusiastic. We finished our drinks and got up.

"I think I'll pick up a bottle of wine," I said.

"That'll pass the time."

I ignored this quip. In fact, I wanted to be able to offer Lisette a drink. If she didn't get in touch, I'd take the wine home and serve it to Tony with a home-cooked meal.

Tony wandered off while I browsed the alcoholic offerings, which included many more cases of cheap beer than bottles of fine wine. I chose a Cabernet from a local vintner I recognized—one of the better New Mexico wineries—and grabbed a corkscrew from a nearby display, then went to the checkout counter to pay for them. A wiry, grizzled little white guy was there buying a heap of canned goods.

"You got any more beans in the back?" he demanded.

"Just what's on the shelf," said the clerk, a tall, round man. "I think you cleaned us out."

"Y'oughta stock more than this. Winter and a storm's comin'," grumped the old guy, and I recognized his voice. I'd heard it before, much louder, yelling at the cowboys outside the dining hall. He looked smaller than I remembered, no taller than me. I waited patiently while he counted out dollar bills and quarters to pay for his purchase. As he left with his haul, still grumbling, the clerk gave me an apologetic shrug.

"One of the neighbors?" I asked.

"Yeah, he's got some land north of here. Digs holes all over it. He's convinced he'll find gold."

"Everyone needs a dream," I said, and paid for my wine, then went in search of Tony. I found him in the "outdoor equipment" section, frowning at a shelf full of gear.

"Something wrong?" I asked.

He looked at me, then picked up a package of rope. "Ready to go?"

"What's that for?"

He glanced at a woman who was browsing the camping gear nearby. "Tell you later."

8

HAD I NOT KNOWN TONY AS WELL AS I DID, this would have frightened me. Even so, just a tiny stab of fear flashed through me before reason restored my balance. Tony would *never* hurt me, or threaten me.

I looked more closely at the woman. It was the short-haired Anglo woman from the studio tour and the trail ride. And the Ghost House. What was she after?

She didn't look at me. Maybe it was just a small world. Julio liked to say that there were a hundred people in New Mexico, fifty of them lived in Santa Fe, and the rest were extras.

Tony paid for the rope. We returned to the car with tiny snowflakes swirling around us.

"So what's with the rope?" I said as I pulled onto the highway, heading back to Ghost Ranch.

"It looks familiar."

I glanced at him. He was still frowning.

"I had a lot of time to look around the crime scene until the locals arrived," he said. "Had a good look at the body. This looks like the same kind of rope."

I let out a gasp of dismay. "It c-could have come from anywhere, couldn't it?"

"Yeah, but just in case, I wanted to pick this up. CSI can test it, see if it's from the same batch. Might prove the rope was bought from Bode's."

"God."

"Just a minor detail."

That's how a case was built, though. By now, I knew that minor details could add up into solid evidence.

"Tony, are you going to end up working this case?"

"Probably not. Locals are pretty territorial, usually."

"Oh."

"But I'm not sure Rio Arriba has a full-time homicide guy. If they ask, I'll help out."

"Oh."

"It's not likely."

I was silent, playing out scenarios in my mind. Tony saving the day, rescuing the rural cops with his urban know-how. Me...sitting around, waiting.

Good thing I had a book.

Good thing I'd bought the wine.

"When's our dinner reservation, again?" Tony asked as I pulled into my parking space. The Roans' SUV was gone.

"Six-thirty," I said.

"I'll just take this over to the office, in case those guys are still there," he said, hefting the bag with the rope.

"OK."

He opened the door for me, carried in the wine and put it on the dresser, then headed for the welcome center with the rope. I hung up my coat, got out the O'Keeffe biography, and curled up on the bed with it. Soon I was lost in the art world that O'Keeffe had set by the ears. She'd been the first woman in America to be acknowledged a major artist. She'd fought uphill all the way for recognition, and blazed the trail for many woman artists to follow. Not even a century ago, and so much had changed for the better since then. It was good to remember that.

My thoughts strayed to Lisette, a serious student of art before her marriage. She had the additional disadvantage of being black, which in O'Keeffe's day would probably have deprived her even of the opportunity to study art. I hoped she would continue to draw and paint, going forward. It might prove to be her salvation.

My phone buzzed with an incoming text. Tony, I thought, and wondered as I reached for the phone if he was going to excuse himself. I wouldn't be surprised if he was hobnobbing with the "locals." The clock showed an hour had passed since I'd started reading.

Instead of Tony's name, I saw an unfamiliar phone number at

the head of the message:

Why didn't you tell me
you found him?

I set the book aside.

Lisette?

You knew it was him.

I wasn't sure. I didn't want
to scare you.

Silence. I could picture her: hurt, angry, frightened and confused. My heart went out to her.

You want to come over
and talk? Tony's out.

Silence again. I tried to think of a way to coax her over. Tea? Wine? I envisioned her haughty refusal—a wounded soul taking comfort in defiance.

Lisette, I'm sorry if I've
angered you. It's been a
terrible day. If you'd like to
talk, I'm here. If not, I
understand.

Best I could do. I waited a moment, then set the phone down and picked up my book. I'd tried to read the same paragraph three times by the time my phone buzzed again.

I'm coming.

I jumped up and tidied the room, which didn't really need much tidying. Still, I couldn't concentrate on the book. I put it on the dresser and collected the two mugs from the bathroom where I'd left them to dry after washing them. Tea or wine; they'd serve either way. I took them into the Room of Many Chairs.

A knock fell on the door, so quiet I almost missed it. I opened it to Lisette, shades on, hair hidden under a scarf, mouth in a straight line. Her hands were tucked in the pockets of her leather jacket.

"Come in," I said, stepping back.

She did so. I offered to take her jacket, but she shook her

head. "It's cold."

"I can make tea, if you like. Or I have some wine."

Her head lifted slightly and the line of her mouth became thinner. "Tea," she said after a pause.

"Make yourself at home," I said, then fetched the kettle and went to fill it from the sink. When I returned, Lisette was sitting on the foot of the our bed. I went into the other room, set the kettle to heat, then returned.

"How's Jeremy?"

"Sleeping. I gave him a pill."

"He seemed pretty shaken."

"Are you surprised?" Her voice was brittle with anger and pain.

"No, of course not," I said softly. I sat on the foot of the bed, facing her. "Lisette, I'm sorry I couldn't tell you everything right away. Even if I'd been sure, I wouldn't have been able to tell you."

She shifted, angling her body toward me. Listening, but conceding nothing.

"I'm so sorry," I added. "If I can help, I'd like to."

"You know they think I did it."

"Everyone's a suspect at the start," I said. "They interviewed me, too, just because I spotted…because I saw him first."

"Did you tell them he hit me?"

"No."

She seemed to relax a little. The kettle boiled, and I made tea. When I brought her a mug, she drew her hands out of her pockets at last, and held the mug in both hands like a child, taking hesitant sips.

"This is such good tea," she whispered.

I fetched my own mug and sat with her in silence for a while, feeling oddly tired. It was emotional, rather than physical, exhaustion. Lisette must feel even more drained.

"Don't worry," I said. "They'll find the killer."

"I don't care if they find him. I just want them to leave me alone."

I stopped myself from assuring her they would. She was black, and from Texas. In her world, cops were likely to kill for no reason. I couldn't promise her that the "locals" here would be any different, especially knowing the animosity that was typical between blacks and Hispanics in this state.

As if aware of my thoughts, she added, "They won't let me go home."

"I'm sure that's temporary," I said, though I actually wasn't sure.

"I want to send Jeremy home, but they won't let me do that either," she said, anger growling low through her voice. "They're suspicious of him, too. An eleven-year-old boy. He cried for an hour after that...man...talked to him."

"I'm so sorry," was all I could say.

"All the times I prayed to be free from my marriage," she whispered, shaking her head. "I never thought it would be worse with him gone, but it is."

"It'll get better," It sounded lame even as I said it. I tried again. "Just take one day at a time. One task at a time. Focus on one thing you can do something about. The rest will work itself out."

She turned her head toward me. "You've never been where I am now."

"No, but I've been in bad situations. You'll get through it. You're strong."

The sound of the outer door's keypad made us both jump. I stood, moving toward the door, placing myself between it and Lisette. Same as before, I realized.

Tony stepped in. He looked about to speak, but caught my nod toward Lisette and hesitated.

"Ma'am," he said gently.

Lisette stood. "I'll be going. Thank you for the tea."

She held out her mug. I accepted it.

"You'll be all right?" I phrased it as a question, though I wanted her to know it was a fact.

"Yes."

The shield was back. Warrior Mom, determined to show no weakness. She brushed past Tony on her way out the door.

"Call me if you need anything," I said.

"Let me walk you to your room," Tony said simultaneously.

Lisette stiffened. "Thanks, but I'm fine."

"Please, ma'am," Tony added. "I'll feel better knowing you're safe."

She stared at him, then turned her head toward me.

"I'll come too, if you like," I said.

A swallow moved her throat. "OK," she said.

Conjecture buzzed in my head as I hustled into my coat and hat. Tony's offer was unusually gallant. I had to assume he had reason for concern about Lisette's safety.

Maybe it was just caution. Cops were well-versed in paranoia. Wesley had been killed; the motive could have been more than just a hate crime. If so, Lisette might also be in danger.

And her son.

Snowflakes wafted about as we stepped outside. The thirsty ground was sucking it up. I looked up at the big cottonwoods. One of them was the hanging tree. I glanced at Lisette, glad that I hadn't told her the story. She strode past without looking at them.

We followed her up the path, taking the through branch toward the little parking lot. She walked past the cars to one of the casitas, a nice-looking one with three entrances. She stopped by the center one and turned to us.

"Thank you," she said.

Tony gave a nod. "Keep safe."

"You have my number," I added.

Lisette entered a code in the keypad, opened the door, and went in. Shutting the door quite loudly. Tony was still for a moment, then turned back toward the path.

I decided to wait until we were back inside before making conversation. As we walked down the hill I pondered whether to ask Tony why he'd insisted on walking Lisette home. Had he heard something? Picked up on hostility from the sheriffs?

In the end, I merely thanked him. "She's kind of brittle right now. I hope you weren't offended."

He gave me an amused look. "I can tell defensive behavior from offensive attitude."

"You think she's at risk."

"She could be."

I shrugged out of my coat and went to hang it up. "You were away for a while."

Tony reached for a hanger. "The locals wanted my take on the vic."

"Vic?"

"The victim. Roan."

"Oh." I fetched the mugs and took them to the sink to wash,

remembering Tony's cold fury at the O'Keeffe studio. "Did you tell them he insulted you?"

"Yeah. They weren't surprised. He insulted a lot of people."

I collected the teapot and the infuser, from which I dumped out the wet tea leaves. "I wonder why he was so full of spite."

Tony leaned against the door frame, watching me wash the mugs. "Bad childhood, maybe. Turned him into a bully. The kind of guy who doesn't know any way to feel powerful other than stomping other people down."

"So we have an idea why he was killed. But not who did it."

"Lot of candidates."

I put the mugs on a clean washcloth to dry, rinsed out the teapot and cleaned the infuser, sat on the bed to take off my shoes. Tony joined me.

"In order to narrow the field, do you look at who is physically capable of subduing a man that big?" I asked.

He tilted his head, looking slightly bemused. "That's one factor."

"The only one I can think of is the guy in the flag cap. Maybe."

"It's more complicated than that."

I waited for him to elaborate. He returned my gaze, then looked away, frowning a little.

"You have to treat this like one of my cases," he said at last. "Total confidentiality."

"All right."

"That means you don't share anything with Mrs. Roan."

"OK."

"I know you think she's innocent."

"I'm pretty sure of it, but I won't tell her anything you share. I thought you were concerned for her safety?"

"I am, but she's also a flight risk."

"Tony!"

"Gotta go by the rules."

I took a calming breath. "She complained that they wouldn't let her go home," I said carefully. "To me, that indicates she's *abiding* by the rules."

He gazed at me briefly, then sighed. "Roan wasn't just hanged," he said. "There's more to it. And it wasn't the hanging that killed him."

I blinked. My assumptions about the crime shattered. I'd

pictured a lynch mob, because I couldn't think of any other way for it to happen.

"How do you know?"

Tony took out his phone, poked at it, then handed it to me. It was showing a photo of the ground.

"What do you see?"

I peered at it. The soil was soft, like in the bottom of an arroyo. Differences in height cast long shadows, even though the contrast wasn't strong. There were tire tracks, with a footprint impressed deeply over them.

"Is this…the arroyo?" I asked.

"Yeah. I took some pictures while I was waiting."

"Is that Mr. Roan's footprint?"

"It matches his shoes."

"So a vehicle was there, then he walked over the tracks."

"Yes. The vehicle track is old, actually. See how soft it is?"

I nodded.

"What else do you see?"

I pointed to the lower left corner of the photo. "I think that's a hoofprint."

"Yes."

"And there's another footprint under the hoofprint."

"Good. What else?"

I frowned. "There are streaks."

"Yes."

"They go partly across the hoofprint. It almost looks like someone swept."

"Bingo. They dragged a branch, actually."

I looked up at him. "So someone was trying to cover up the tracks?"

Tony nodded. "But it was dark, so they missed a couple. Actually, they missed a lot, because he went out there on foot. But they did obscure most of the marks at the scene."

I handed back the phone and stared at the wall, picturing the killer at the crime scene. Darkness. A hanging. Brushing away tracks with a branch. And Tony had implied there was more.

"It was dark," I repeated.

"Yeah. Time of death estimate is around eight p.m."

"While we were at the concert."

"Yes. That's my alibi, thank you."

"Oh, Tony!" I turned to hug him. "They can't seriously think you're a suspect."

"They have to consider everyone. The guy did address a racial slur to me, in front of witnesses."

I buried my head in his shoulder. The same gesture I'd seen Jeremy do with his mom. "They know it wasn't you."

"I think they do. But they have to check every possibility. So thank you for dragging me to that concert."

I looked up at him. "You didn't want to watch more football anyway."

"With that asshole around? No way."

I laughed, though it made me feel guilty. Asshole or no, the man was dead.

I tucked my feet up under me. Tony stretched out and leaned against the pillows, hands behind his head.

"What was Wesley doing walking around out in the arroyo?" I said. "It's so far from the ranch!"

"He wasn't a weakling," Tony said. "According to his son, he liked to run, though he wasn't regular about it. They found his tracks going in along the service road, and it looked more like jogging than walking. We figure he ran most of the way. We just don't know why."

I took a breath. "I might be able to help with that."

"Oh, yeah?"

I stood and paced to the window. The snow was starting to fall more densely. I didn't want to betray Lisette's confidence, and I certainly didn't want to give the police any reason to suspect her more than they already did. But I thought I could guess why Wesley ran out so far from the ranch.

"He had an argument with his wife," I said, turning to face Tony.

"A fight?"

"She bought some art supplies and was drawing with them. He didn't like it." I chose carefully how to put it: I wanted to be truthful, but still protect Lisette's privacy. "She told me he tore up her picture, then stormed out."

He sat up. "This was last night?"

"So I gathered."

"Did you tell the locals?"

"No. They didn't ask. I assumed she'd tell them, when they

asked her where she was yesterday evening."

Tony frowned. "That could be considered withholding evidence."

I shook my head. "It's incidental. We already knew that he was abusive toward his family. A torn picture isn't a likely motive for murder. But it could explain why he ran off, to blow off steam."

Tony sighed. "What else did she say?"

I gazed at him for a long moment. "She didn't tell me this, but I observed something. I want you to keep it in confidence."

"If it has a bearing on the crime, I can't."

"Then you'll have to make your own observations."

He gave me a flat look. "You're not being objective. You're protecting her."

"I'm protecting her because I see her being unfairly targeted! Tony, she's not the kind of person to kill a man."

"*Anyone* can become a killer."

"She has a son to take care of. Given Wesley's behavior toward Jeremy, I think she'd have killed him long ago if she'd wanted to, and been able to."

Tony's eyes narrowed. "What if Wesley threatened the boy's life yesterday?"

"I agree, that would be an inspiring motive. But I don't think Jeremy was there when Wesley tore up the painting. Lisette didn't mention him."

Tony gave a grudging nod. "You're right. He was in the cantina, watching TV, from seven to around ten. Lots of people corroborated it."

"So Jeremy wasn't under any threat," I said.

"And he probably didn't kill his dad."

I came back to the bed and curled up against Tony. He slid his free arm around me. I snuggled against him, comforted by the contact.

"Lisette and Wesley were alone when he tore up her picture," I said. "Why would she follow him to kill him over that? And I bet she's not able to run as fast as he could. She's trim, but all her shoes are more fashionable than practical. She's not an athlete."

Tony was silent. I turned to face him. "Were there any footprints that could be hers? On the road, following his?"

"No. But that just means she didn't go in on foot."

"If she'd gone in a vehicle, the tracks would cover some of his."

"True. We didn't spot any like that, but we didn't walk the whole length of the road."

"And now the snow is covering the tracks."

"Might still be something to see, once it melts."

"*If* it melts."

"Let's check the forecast."

Tony picked up his phone and swiped at it. I thought of Lisette, alone in her room with her sleeping son. I hadn't asked, but I guessed that she didn't have an alibi. She'd just been through an argument and been hit by her husband. She probably didn't feel like going out. Maybe she took a shower. Maybe she went to bed, with an icepack for her eye. Either way, no alibi.

I wished I could offer her more comfort, though I had to respect her wishes and her need for privacy. Did her casita have a fireplace, I wondered? If it was a kiva fireplace, did she know how to light a fire in it? Probably not.

But then, it was probably blocked up with particle board anyway.

"Hmm," Tony said. "Doesn't look good. Eight to ten inches."

"*Tonight?*"

"According to the weather site. Mostly after midnight. Looks like we might get snowed in, babe."

I pictured trying to get my Camry down the dirt entrance road in eight inches of snow. "Maybe the ranch has a plow blade for one of their trucks," I said hopefully.

Looking toward the window, I saw it was beginning to get dark. Suddenly I wasn't sure we'd be able to drive to the Inn for our dinner reservation, or more importantly, to get back. I got up and walked over to the window, peering at the gray sky. The snow was falling harder, starting to stick. Maybe a quarter inch on the ground.

"Let me show you something," Tony said.

I went back to the bed. He handed me his phone. "There was one other print at the scene. Smaller than Roan's. I spotted it near the edge of the arroyo."

More dirt, a couple of scraggy clumps of dry grass, a tree branch. At the edge of a grass clump, the back half of a boot print: flat and without tread, but with a heel.

"Could be a cowboy boot," I said.

"Looks like it."

"Lisette wasn't wearing cowboy boots on the trail ride."

"I know."

"So this probably isn't her print."

"Yeah."

There had to be a zillion cowboy boots in Rio Arriba County. I frowned, then zoomed in the picture. "The end of that branch has been cut."

"Very good. That's the branch that was dragged over the prints."

"So you could get a fingerprint from it!"

"Not likely, off of bark. And the killer could have worn gloves."

"But they'll look at it?"

"Yup. Evidence guys collected it."

I frowned. "That's the only other footprint?"

"I think so." Tony nodded toward the phone. "I took more pictures. Go ahead and look at them. Maybe you'll see something I didn't."

I scrolled through, a little worried that there would be a picture of the scene that was already etched on my memory. Most were pictures of dirt, with more streaks of the branches. I squinted, but couldn't make out any footprints. Pictures of the arroyo as it continued northward. A picture of a fence across the arroyo, with a hand-painted sign hanging on it, blue with white letters, like the sign I'd seen on the trail ride. Pictures of trees. Pictures of the view back toward the place where the horse trail crossed the arroyo.

I handed the phone back to Tony, and sat musing. "You said he wasn't just hanged."

"No."

"What else?"

"Sure you want to hear?"

I looked at him. His face was serious. The concerned face; he wanted to protect me.

"If I can help, then yes," I said.

"He was dragged behind the horse before he was strung up."

Dragged?

"Yeah. The killer brushed away most of the marks, but they

didn't brush the dirt off his back, and his clothes were messed up. They put the rope under his arms, dragged him to the tree, and strung him up."

I was appalled. I'd assumed it was a hate crime, but now it looked even worse.

"So he was unconscious? Or were his hands tied?"

"Hands weren't tied. He took a blow to the head, so probably unconscious."

"God."

"Also..."

"What?"

"He was shot. With a shotgun."

I blinked, and took a steadying breath. "Before or after he was hanged?"

"Good question. After, they think—because he didn't bleed much. It wasn't point blank, so the shot scattered."

"They shot him after he was dead? Just for spite?"

"Looks that way. The MI will know for sure."

I shook my head. I had trouble believing anyone could be so hateful, even to a man like Wesley Roan.

I lived a sheltered life, I knew. I was being shown just how sheltered. Just how awful other people's lives could be. Had been.

Poor Lisette. I wondered how much of this she knew.

"I doubt Lisette has a shotgun," I remarked.

"Wesley could have."

"There's no gun rack in their SUV. And I seriously doubt Lisette would have taken her kid on a trail ride the morning after killing his dad," I said.

"Good point. That would take nerves of steel. Not sure she's that chill."

Suddenly I felt the need to move. I started putting my shoes back on. "Let's go for a walk."

"Where?"

"Anywhere."

"Um, it's still snowing...."

I put on my coat and pulled my scarf out of the pockets, then grabbed my hat off the dresser. Tony got up and fetched his own coat and hat.

Outside, I took deep breaths of the clean, cold air. Tony stood beside me, waiting. Giving me the lead. I looked toward the dining hall, where there was coffee but not much else at this hour. Looked back toward the welcome center, but thought the sheriffs might still be around.

"Show me the cantina," I said.

"OK."

He led the way up the road past the dining hall. We passed a large dorm building, L-shaped with a big yard in front. Beyond it was a long, unmarked building. Tony led me to the left end, where there was a door.

"This is it?"

"Yeah. Shh. There are probably people watching a game."

After just that short walk, my face was chilled and I needed to blow my nose. We brushed the snow off our shoulders, stamped it off our feet, then went in.

I had expected something remotely lounge-like, perhaps with a couple of old sofas. Instead, we entered a room with an old TV in a cabinet in one corner and a large kiva fireplace in another, its mouth blocked with the usual particle board. A spinet-style piano near the door looked pathetically lonely, and rang more summer camp bells. Several people sat in a semi-circle of folding chairs, watching the football game on TV and listening to the sports announcer's commentary through its single, tinny speaker. The only person I recognized was the flag hat guy. Today he had on a Cowboys sweatshirt as well as the hat (which he shouldn't have been wearing indoors). He gave me a long look, glanced at Tony, and returned his attention to the TV. The program appeared to be a pregame show—lots of talk, with occasional clips from various football games.

I could just imagine Wesley Roan's indignation on being presented with this room as the best option for viewing The Game.

Tony helped me out of my coat, and hung it on a coat rack along with his. He led the way over to two empty chairs at the end of the semicircle. I sat beside him, watched the commentary for a couple of minutes, then snuck a look at Flag-Hat Guy. He was probably around forty, white as could be, with a light sprinkling of freckles to go with his sandy hair. He held a beer can in one hand, and occasionally dipped the other into a bag of barbecue-flavored chips on the chair next to his.

Could this be a man who had killed the previous night? If he was, he was a consummate actor, because he looked entirely blasé. Killing time—so to speak—until the game began.

"Dang, it's quiet," said a pudgy man with brown hair.

"Be grateful," said a heavily tanned guy with bristly gray hair across the room. "Every minute that Texans jerk stays away is a gift."

"Figured he'd be here by now," said the pudgy guy.

I kept my attention on Flag Hat Guy. He'd heard this exchange, because he'd glanced once at the pudgy guy. But his face showed no reaction. He didn't suddenly flush (as redheads were prone to do). He didn't fidget in his chair. He was merely bored, merely waiting. I found this disappointing, since Flag Hat Guy was my first choice for a murder suspect.

"He won't be coming," Tony said, which surprised me. Everyone turned to look at him. I shifted my gaze to the side, so Flag Hat wouldn't catch me watching him. He glanced at Tony, then looked back at the TV. Still bored.

"He a friend of yours?" asked the pudgy guy.

"No," Tony said. "I just know he won't be here."

"How come?"

"'Cause he died last night."

9

SUDDENLY ALL EYES WERE ON US. Tony had surprised me as much as the others, and I looked at him with a little gasp.

"Ha! Best news I heard all day!"

It was Flag Hat. I shot him a resentful glance, but he wasn't looking. He was swigging his beer.

"What happened?" asked the tanned guy.

Tony was looking at his phone, apparently deaf. He stood and turned to me, holding out a hand. "Gotta go."

Embarrassed, I glanced around the room, then let him lead me away. We retrieved our coats and donned them on the way out the door.

"Why did you say that?" I hissed.

Tony grinned, but didn't answer.

"They're going to think we're weird, leaving right after we got there," I said as we trudged away.

"You didn't really want to watch football, did you?" Tony said.

"No."

The sky was thickening overhead. It was still daylight, but the storm was heavy enough that it was hard to tell the time of day. The sun was completely obscured. The snowfall was getting heavier, and cast a blanket of quiet over the land.

"Why did you tell them Wesley was dead?" I asked as we passed the dining hall.

"Flushing the wolf out of the sheep pen, I hope."

"But now they're going to spread the word, and go looking for information!"

"Right. And the ones who *don't* go looking, might be worth looking at."

I digested that for a few paces. "What are the 'locals' going to think of your strategy?"

"If it's successful, they'll be grateful, I hope. Think I'll walk down to HQ and hang out for a while, see if anyone takes the bait."

"I'll go with you."

"You don't have to."

"Better than sitting around doing nothing."

We had maybe an hour before we should get ready for our dinner at the Abiquiu Inn. If Tony was going to spend it hobnobbing with "the locals," I sure wasn't going to spend it sitting around in our room.

In the welcome center, situation normal. The trading post was open, the snack bar closed with a sign referring the hungry to the trading post. Tony took a quick look around, then headed for the office the sheriffs had used for interviews. I wandered into the trading post, where I recognized one of the middle-aged ladies who'd been on our trail ride, buying a Ghost Ranch sweatshirt and a scarf.

The center of the shop was filled with racks of souvenir clothing and shelves of knick-knacks and snacks. One long wall displayed books, and at the end was a section of art supplies. This was where Lisette had bought her pastels. I looked them over. Bound pads and spiral-bound books of drawing paper in several sizes, sets of pastels and watercolors, brushes, even "how to paint" books. Everything for the beginner inspired by O'Keeffe's landscapes.

I tried to recall any work of hers that featured snow. Couldn't come up with one. Glancing up, I looked over a collection of O'Keeffe posters hung just under a high set of clerestory windows. Most were of the local landscapes. Only one jumped out at me, *Black Cross New Mexico.*

I swallowed, not wanting to contemplate that particular image at the moment. I went back to the books, looking for a big fat book filled with reproductions of O'Keeffe's art, something I'd been wishing I had as I read the biography, which was filled with references to specific paintings. Several such books were offered, all prohibitively expensive. I picked one of them and checked the index for "snow." No luck. Leafing through the book, which was roughly in chronological order, I saw the progression of her work from the early years in New York—the city views and the wildly successful flower paintings—to Lake George where she'd spent summers with Alfred Stieglitz's family, to Texas where she'd taught art for a while, and ultimately to New Mexico. Once she'd discovered Taos, and then the Chama River valley, it was all over. This was where she wanted to be, and not even her marriage to Stieglitz which by then was on the rocks—could keep her away.

In fact, finding Ghost Ranch had rescued her from a bout of chronic depression that had followed an unpleasant discovery: Stieglitz had been having an affair with his assistant. Though O'Keeffe remained in the marriage until Stieglitz died, her work took precedence ever after.

I wondered if Tony's work would take precedence. Not that I would ever cheat on him—but I sometimes felt he was jealous of the energy and attention I spent on the tearoom. Having made a serious commitment to my career, I had to consider that Tony's devotion to his work was every bit as serious. I'd have to be prepared for the possibility that his job would, at least sometimes, take precedence. Would our marriage succeed anyway? Would it be worth the effort to make it succeed?

Turning a page, I saw a familiar painting: *From the Faraway Nearby.* Not snow, exactly, but it had a wintry look. The giant, antlered skull—I suspected elk, rather than deer—points reaching skyward against a background that went from pale pink to vibrant blue, reminded me of the barren trees in the river valley. The hills on the horizon were tiny, almost an afterthought, compared to the antlers that dominated the picture. O'Keeffe had even added an extra antler branch to the left side of the arrangement, which I'd never noticed before, despite staring at Mom's poster since my childhood.

Strange, the things we fail to notice, even though they're right before us.

I closed the book and put it back on the shelf. Maybe the Ranch's library would have a copy I could borrow. I continued browsing the books, and heard a woman's voice behind me complaining that her sunset tour had been canceled.

"Well, honey," said another woman, "ain't going to see no sunset today, and you wouldn't like riding a horse through this snow."

Not to mention that it would hardly be safe, going up and down the narrow paths in and out of the arroyos. And there would be no breathtaking views.

I glanced behind me to see who was speaking. A party of four women I didn't recognize—new arrivals, maybe—nursing cups of hot coffee from the snack bar as they groused. They looked like tourists, wearing heavy flannel shirts and down vests, and cowboy boots that looked brand new. They didn't know how lucky they were that their excursion had been canceled—an hour and a half in the saddle in unbroken boots—yikes!

I turned to the nick-knacks, thinking I should choose some little gifts for my friends and staff. Kris would be easy—something with the cow-skull Ghost Ranch logo on it, preferably black. Of course, I already had O'Keeffe's favorite tea for her, but I felt kind of obligated to get something with the cow skull as well. For Nat, I had the O'Keeffe datebook. For Julio, Manny, and Gina, it was a harder choice. I browsed my way around the end of a shelf, started going up the other side, and stopped.

There, talking rather earnestly to the cashier, was the older, tanned guy who'd been in the cantina. I couldn't hear what he was saying. Casually browsing, pretending interest in the T-shirts and souvenir shot glasses, I gradually sidled closer to the cash register, keeping my back toward it as much as possible in case the tanned guy remembered me.

"—said the guy was dead, but didn't say how."

"Yeah, he's dead," said the cashier. "The cops are here."

"Any idea what happened?"

"No, but they're talking to people. Must have been a fight."

I paused next to the shot glasses and took out my phone to send Tony a text:

> Guy from cantina in trading
> post. Asking clerk about
> Wesley.

Turning away, I pocketed my phone and ambled out toward the office where the sheriffs had been. The door was closed. I didn't see Tony; maybe he was inside, conferring.

It was cold in the entryway, so I went into the reception room, where a solitary clerk was sitting behind the counter waiting to assist anyone who braved the snow to get here. It was the same woman who'd checked us in and told me about the Ghost House: Debbie. We exchanged nods. She seemed a little tense, but given the events of the past few hours, that was understandable.

"I hope everyone's here who needs to be," I said, glancing toward the window.

"There's one party coming in, but they might cancel. All the tours are canceled anyway."

I nodded and sipped. "Do you live in Abiquiu?"

"Tesuque."

"How's the highway?"

"I came it at seven, so I don't know. Shouldn't be too bad yet."

I heard a door close, and glanced toward the hall. Tony had come out of the office and was heading for the trading post. I turned back to Debbie.

"I really enjoyed the concert last night. Does Bernardo Milagro play here very often?"

"Usually once a year. It almost always sells out. Last night didn't, but January's pretty slow."

"Well, I'll probably come again. He was amazing."

"He does workshops, too. Here, they're in the catalog."

She offered me a brochure listing the (expensive) classes, workshops, and retreats available throughout the year. I already had a copy, but I accepted it with a smile and listened to her describe Milagro's "Sacred Drumming" workshop. Tony came in just as she was wrapping up.

"There you are."

"Hi," I said as Tony slid his arm around my waist and pulled me toward the hall. "The deputy wants to talk to you," he said quietly when we were out.

"Again?"

My heart gave a little flutter of cop aversion. I told it to settle down. I had nothing to fear, and nothing to hide.

Same office, but this time it was the younger sheriff behind the desk. He stood as I came in, and offered a hand.

"Ms. Rosings? I'm Victor Trujillo."

"Hello."

His handshake was feather-light. He invited me politely to sit, and as I looked closer at his face I began to wonder if he might be Pueblo, or part Pueblo. The rounded cheeks, the narrow eyes—and his gentle demeanor was strikingly different from that of his colleague. And there was definitely something familiar about him, but I couldn't pinpoint it. His black hair was cut fairly short, but not buzzed.

Tony had come in with me, and took the other visitor chair, pushing it back so he could see both me and the sheriff. I wondered where the older guy was.

"I was expecting Sheriff Romero," I said into the silence.

Trujillo and Tony exchanged a wry glance. "He's gone home for the day. But this case is still a priority, so I'll be here for a while."

Trujillo was probably a bachelor, then, and Romero went home to his family, leaving the mess in his subordinate's hands. I glanced at Tony. Clearly he was comfortable with this guy, which told me a lot.

"How can I help you?" I said as the silence stretched again. I knew it was a classic cop technique, but Trujillo didn't seem to want to intimidate me. More like he was waiting for me to think of something new.

"Would you mind just going over what happened yesterday again?" he said, leaning his elbows on the desk and lacing his fingers together. "Sorry, but I wasn't here for your interview. All I have is my boss's notes." He gestured toward the open file before him, and I remembered how laboriously the sheriff had written. Highly likely that he hadn't recorded everything I said.

"OK," I said, and proceeded to tell him the whole story. His expression was of mild interest, and I found myself offering more detail, incidental as it might be. Occasionally he nodded, but he didn't say anything until I had finished.

"Do you think any of the others saw the body?" he asked.

"If they did, they didn't say anything. Tony and I were at the end of the string."

He nodded, and made a couple of notes on a steno pad, then put down the pen and looked at me. "I understand you're acquainted with the Roan family?"

"Just with Lisette, really. I haven't talked much with Jeremy, and not at all with Wesley."

Slow nod. "How did you meet Mrs. Roan?"

"At the drinks counter in the dining hall."

"The drinks counter?"

"Yes. We struck up a conversation and discovered we both

like tea."

"Ah."

He gazed at the desktop, as if contemplating tea. I sat back in my chair, perfectly willing to wait.

"Did Mrs. Roan seem happy to you?" he asked after a pause.

"Happy?"

"When you met."

I thought about it, then sighed. "I wouldn't describe her as happy, no. Resigned, perhaps."

"Resigned? To her marriage?"

"Best to be hoped for, really."

"With a husband like Mr. Roan, you mean."

I nodded.

"Do you think she wanted out of her marriage?"

I paused. Lisette had told me as much, but not until today. Had I thought she wanted out yesterday?

"Probably," I said. "It wasn't a good match."

"Then why did they get married?"

"He wanted a pretty wife, she wanted security."

"But then—somewhere along the way—she changed her mind?"

I returned his placid gaze, wondering if he was gently laying a trap for me. "I don't know that," I said slowly, "but I wouldn't be surprised to hear it."

"But she didn't get a divorce."

"They have a son. Maybe she stayed for his sake."

"Did she tell you that?"

"No," I said, "but she did tell me she was going to make sure Jeremy had opportunities his father never had."

Trujillo lifted his chin slightly. "Wasn't Mr. Roan well off?"

"Apparently. His wife is certainly well-dressed. They have a luxurious car."

"You've seen their car?"

"Lisette gave me a ride back in it, after the trail ride."

When Tony was with *you,* I added in thought. Going over the crime scene.

I looked at Tony, who was kicked back in his chair, listening. He gave me a tiny shrug.

"She gave you a ride back," Trujillo said. "Did you mention what you had seen?"

I straightened in my chair. "I know better than that," I said, matching his gentle tone.

"You didn't say anything at all?"

"I told her that I'd seen what might be a crime scene, and that I couldn't talk about it."

"OK." He nodded. "What about later? After she knew?"

"After she knew, she chewed me out for not telling her before."

"Oh." He looked at his pen, but didn't pick it up. Instead, he met my gaze again. "Do you think she's innocent?"

"I do."

"She has no alibi."

"That's understandable."

He looked surprised. "Understandable?"

"She stayed in the room alone after they argued and he stormed away."

A slight frown creased his forehead. "Why is that understandable?"

I took a steadying breath. I'd said as much as I dared, as much as I felt I was obligated to. "Have you talked to her, Sheriff Trujillo?"

"Deputy. No, I haven't."

"When you do, be as considerate as you've been toward me, and you should learn some things."

His eyes widened slightly, then he gave a slow nod. "Thank you."

I nodded back.

As if this signaled the end of the interview, Tony sat up and stretched. "Think I'll go see what people are gossiping about."

Trujillo stood as well, and they exchanged a light fist bump. He then turned to me.

"Thank you, Ms. Rosings. I might want to talk with you again."

"Sure," I said, shaking hands. Again, he barely touched my fingers. "I'm happy to help any way I can."

He smiled, then sat and picked up his pen. Tony held the door for me. Glancing toward the front doors as we entered the hall, I saw that the sky was darker. Snow coming down harder.

Tony headed for the snack bar, where the four newcomers had settled in with their coffee and were passing around a package of cookies from the trading post. They had progressed from grousing about their canceled tour to grousing about the snow. Tony made a slow circuit of the room, apparently admiring the movie posters, though I was sure he was eavesdropping shamelessly. Unwilling to join this masquerade, I took out my phone. It was after five.

In a couple of minutes, Tony joined me and led the way toward the front doors. Before stepping out, I wound my scarf around my neck and zipped up my coat. Hat on head, gloves on hands because the snow was about an inch deep and we had to go down the uneven path.

The storm had brought darkness early. The parking area below was lit by a couple of tall lights. Snowflakes danced through the orangish light and back into the dark. Tony stayed beside me as we walked slowly back to the Ghost House. There were a few footprints in the snow, already getting covered up.

At our door, we de-snowed ourselves as much as possible before going in. Tony unlocked it and I stepped in.

"Babe, I think we're gonna have to postpone that fancy dinner," he said, nudging the thermostat on the wall up a tick.

"Yeah," I said, shaking snow from my hat. "I don't want to drive in this."

"And I want to see what goes on in the dining hall tonight."

I looked up at him. "I get the impression you're actually working the case."

"Unofficially. I offered to back Trujillo up. He was grateful."

"You like him."

Tony shrugged out of his jacket. "He's a good investigator. Better than his boss. He's wasted up here."

I my coat on the back of one of the many chairs, then called the Abiquiu Inn and canceled our dinner reservation, with regrets. The woman on the phone sounded unsurprised.

We had about twenty minutes until the dining hall opened. Tony stretched out on the bed, scrolling through his phone. I wandered over to the dresser and picked up the bottle of wine I'd bought.

"I don't suppose they'd approve of my bringing this to dinner."

"Let's save it for later."

Nodding, I put the bottle down. If we saw Lisette in the dining hall, I might invite her to share it. She'd probably decline if her earlier reaction was any indication, but I wanted to keep in touch with her, keep assuring her that I was a friend.

I looked at Tony. "Do you have any idea where Wesley's money came from?"

"His dad owned a sports bar. He inherited it, then bought two more."

"Oh. Did he argue with his customers like he argued here?"

"His customers were probably all Texans fans. The bars are in Houston."

"So now they're Lisette's."

"Maybe. Depends on his will."

Slightly shocked, I stared. "He wouldn't leave them to someone else!"

"Might leave them to the kid."

"Well, an eleven-year-old can't operate bars. She's Jeremy's legal guardian, so she'd effectively be the owner."

"Maybe."

All these maybes were unsettling. Tony's speculations weren't very likely, I told myself. It would take serious spite to do something like that—leave the bars to his son, leaving Lisette with nothing. Wesley's spite had seemed more...offhanded? Just a habit?

I thought back to the unpleasant exchanges at the O'Keeffe house. Memory had elevated the importance of Wesley's bullying his son, but there had been other moments...how spitefully had I seen him behave toward Lisette? How angry had she been? I tried to remember, back past all the drama and emotion of today.

I joined Tony on the bed. He set his phone down and rolled me into his arms.

"Don't strain your brain. Trujillo's gonna sort that stuff out."

I sighed. "You're right. I'm just worried about Lisette."

"Why don't you text her and offer to walk her to the dining hall?"

I raised myself onto my elbow to look at him. "You think she's in danger, don't you?"

"It's a possibility. If Roan was killed by someone who was after his money—"

"Someone from Texas? But the Roans would have noticed if such a person was here."

"Not if the person was careful. They could be staying at the Inn, or in Española."

"Maybe," I said.

Tony looked up at me with a grin. "I didn't say it was probable. I said it was *possible.*"

I sighed. "I still think Flag Hat Guy is your best bet. Him, or a posse."

Tony shrugged. "Or a hit man."

I stared at him. That hadn't even occurred to me. Of course, it would have to be considered. Probably a standard question in the homicide detective handbook. And, sadly, it removed my objection that Lisette wasn't physically capable of subduing her husband.

I rolled onto my back and stared at the wooden beams of the ceiling. Was Lisette's life with Wesley bad enough that she'd pay to have him killed? It hurt me to ponder that question, because, after all my protests, I suspected the answer was *maybe.*

"You gonna text her?" Tony said. "It's almost quarter to six."

"Yes." I sat up, found my phone, and composed a quick text:

> Tony and I would be happy
> to escort you to dinner.

I should have said "walk," I thought as I slid off the bed and fetched my coat. Tony got up also. By the time we'd bundled up, Lisette still hadn't answered.

"Let's just walk up there," I said. "Maybe we'll meet her on the way."

I braced myself for wind and cold. Instead, when we stepped out, it was into a soft, silent wonderland. Big, fluffy flakes fell past the golden glow of our porch light. The snow-laden sky had a faint glow of its own, slightly pink, though the sun had set by now. Tony turned his phone on flashlight mode and lit the way as we walked up to the parking lot. I couldn't help remembering Christmas Eve, when we'd walked up Canyon Road in the snow, and Tony had blurted out his proposal.

Smiling, I slid my hand into his elbow. Snow was piling up on the Roans' SUV and two other cars in the little parking lot. As we neared Lisette's casita, a figure stepped out of the central door, silhouetted against the glow of the porch light.

A man's figure. Tall, wearing a cowboy hat.

10

I SQUEEZED TONY'S ARM AND STOPPED WALKING. The flashlight disappeared as he shoved his phone into his pocket. The figure started toward us.

What do we do? My heart began hammering. I glanced at the cars. We could go to one of them, start brushing the snow off it, pretending it was ours.

"Heading for dinner?" the man called softly, and I almost fainted with relief. It was Deputy Trujillo.

"We thought we'd see if Mrs. Roan wanted company on the walk," Tony said.

Trujillo joined us, peering at us from beneath his Stetson. "Good idea. I was just talking with her. She'd probably appreciate the offer." He looked at Tony. "And I'd appreciate your keeping an eye on her."

Tony nodded.

Trujillo shifted his gaze to me. "You knew her husband hit her?"

"She didn't tell me so."

Until I asked.

"I noticed she had a shiner when she took off her shades," I added.

He nodded, then glanced up at the falling snow as he pulled on his gloves. "Probably not gonna get away with shades tonight. Thanks for watching out for her."

"Call you later," Tony told him as the deputy started down the path, following our tracks.

We headed toward the Roans' casita again. "You didn't tell me he'd hit her," Tony said.

"It wasn't my secret to tell. You wouldn't promise me confidentiality."

Tony stopped walking. I turned to face him.

"That could be considered obstruction," he said.

"I invited you to make your own observations," I said. "That's all I felt I could do. She didn't volunteer that he'd hit her."

"You know, it's possible to take the Miss Manners thing too far," he said, sounding annoyed.

My own annoyance flared. "Maybe so, but that's my decision. I don't *owe* you my speculations. And I certainly don't owe them to the local sheriffs!"

"I think Trujillo's on Mrs. Roan's side."

"Yeah? What about his boss?"

He sighed. "Fair enough."

I waited, wondering if this was going to be a stumbling block for us. Tony's face was shadowed, hard to read in the dusk and snow. Finally he took a step toward me.

"Sorry," he said in a low voice. "You're right. I'm not even officially on this case. I shouldn't be pressuring you."

"Thank you," I said.

I turned toward the casita, but Tony's hand on my arm stopped me. He folded me in a hug, and I felt myself relaxing.

"Don't be mad," he said in my ear.

"I'm not."

"You sure?"

I took a breath. "Remember what you said about them that first morning? How he didn't respect her?"

Tony glanced toward the casita. "Yeah."

"Well, I'm asking for your respect. If I think you ought to know something I know, I will tell you. Trust me."

Tony held me at arm's length, gazing at me. "OK," he said finally.

We walked up to the casita. Tony knocked on the middle door, and I called out, "Lisette? It's Ellen and Tony."

The door opened after a brief pause. Lisette, sans shades, looked cautiously out. In the shadows, her shiner was hard to detect.

"We thought you might like company walking to dinner," I

said.

She glanced over her shoulder. "Jeremy's still sleeping."

"Well, we could bring something back for you both."

"Or you could bring something back for him," put in Tony.

She hesitated, then opened the door wider. "Come in. I'll write him a note in case he wakes up."

The room we entered was a sitting room or a small living room, with a sofa, an arm chair, and (to my surprise) a television —a new, large, wide-screen. I wondered if Wesley had actually brought it with him, or more likely, gone to Española and bought it when he found out there wasn't a TV in the room. If so, he'd have been disappointed. No cable here, no satellite, probably not even decent reception with a good old-fashioned antenna.

Lisette sat down in the arm chair with a notepad, leaving us the sofa. I noticed a large pad of art paper with a large box of pastels on top of it, sitting neatly on the coffee table in front of the sofa.

So this was where she'd last seen her husband.

Where she'd last been hit by him.

How long had he been hitting her? She hadn't seemed cowed, like a woman who'd suffered long-term abuse, but then she was very good at hiding her feelings.

I watched her write, noting the long, elegant movements of her hand. Her face was calm now. She was relaxed, I realized. Maybe for the first time since I'd met her.

No, she hadn't seemed cowed, but she'd been tense. Tense and bitter. And resigned? I'd thought so...but Tony had persuaded me to doubt.

Until she invited us in. That wasn't the act of a guilty soul.

Maybe I wasn't any good at this. My heart seemed to be getting in the way of detached observation.

She finished her note and stood. "I'll just be a minute," she said softly as she disappeared through a door in the side wall. Apparently, the room could be combined with the neighboring one. Had the Roans taken all three units in this casita? That would have given them a bathroom to themselves, I realized. Extravagant, but then, that fit with what I knew about them. About Wesley, particularly.

Tony poked at the art supplies. I glanced around the rest of the room, seeking any other object that would give a clue to the personalities of the Roans. All I saw were the kind of decorations we had in our own room.

Lisette returned, carrying a dark green scarf, a long, leather coat, and a cream-colored knit cap. "Still asleep," she said, pulling the hat on low and wrapping the scarf high. She put on the coat and headed for the door. Tony and I hastened to follow.

"Thank you," she said as we started down the path. I noted she was wearing the same low-heeled boots she'd worn for the trail ride. The heels were pretty narrow: not spikes, but sort of a skinny French heel. Not the best shoes for slippery footing. As she minced down the hill, arms in the air for balance, I kept an eye on her, ready to offer a steadying hand.

"Thanks," she said when we reached more level ground. Her breath fogged in the evening air.

The snowflakes were lighter now, I realized. Still falling steadily. On the ground, we were up to a couple of inches.

As we neared the dining hall, the snow was packed down by multiple footprints, coming in from all directions to form one line outside the cafeteria door. A couple of people a few steps ahead of us opened the door to go in, emitting light and a yummy baking smell.

I saw movement in the darkness to my left and froze, on alert. Beside me, Lisette halted as well, and whispered, "What?"

The moving shapes resolved themselves into deer. *Lots* of deer. I counted eight before I lost track. They crossed the road about twenty feet from us, heading for the open field. The last one was a young buck, with six antler points. He paused and stared back at us, looking offended, before following his herd into the field.

"Wow," Lisette said softly.

"You haven't seen them before?" I asked.

She shook her head. "I wish Jeremy had seen them."

"Maybe he'll get a chance."

We entered the cafeteria line. Warmth, light, wonderful food smells. Happy voices chatting, and the staff smiling as they kept the food trays full. I pulled off my gloves and stuffed them in a pocket, then took a plate.

There was pizza along with spaghetti and meatballs, and the perennial salad bar. A kitchen worker slid a fresh tray of pizza into place, cementing my choice. Salad on the side.

We moved out into the dining hall, and I dressed my salad with a nice homemade vinaigrette from the condiments table. A gentle hubbub of voices filled the room. There were plenty of empty seats, and a fire was roaring in the fireplace at the far end. I would have headed straight there, but I glanced at Lisette.

She was standing still, staring at the fireplace. Memories of yesterday, I figured. Then she swallowed and looked at me.

"Where would you like to sit?" I asked.

She nodded toward a table in the middle of the room. Tony headed for it at once, and we set down our plates. Lisette chose a seat with her back to the fireplace, and I took the one beside her, while Tony sat across the table.

"I'm going to get a hot drink," I said. "Can I bring you something?"

"Coffee," Tony said, picking up a piece of pizza.

Lisette joined me and we both picked up mugs. I spotted packets of instant cocoa, which looked good except I knew it would be too sweet. I thought about coffee instead, then grabbed a cocoa packet, emptied half of it into a mug, and added coffee. Instant mocha!

"Oooh, that looks good," Lisette said. I offered her the rest of my cocoa packet, and she made her own mocha. I filled a mug with coffee for Tony and we returned to our table to chow down.

Loud, male voices issued from the food line. I looked up and saw Flag Hat Guy emerge from the line carrying two large, foil-wrapped packages. The pudgy guy and the gossipy tanned guy were with him, also with takeout. Flag Hat set down his packages to fill a thermos mug with coffee while the other two argued about who would win The Game. None of them looked our way.

I became aware of Lisette sitting stiffly, arms clamped to her side, gaze on her plate as she swallowed. Maybe it was just the presence of men who had argued with her husband. Maybe it was the loud voices. Whatever it was, she relaxed a bit when they headed outside with their boxes.

"Guess there's an important game tonight," I remarked.

"Yeah," Tony said. "I might go watch for a while."

Lisette drew a breath, then picked up her pizza and took a bite. I stabbed a forkful of salad.

"I'm not much of a football fan," I remarked. "Too violent for me. Always has been."

Lisette gave me a grateful glance. I smiled back.

"Lisette, do you like wine? I have a bottle, if you'd like to share it. I could bring it to your room if you want to get back to Jeremy."

She paused, frowning slightly. "I do drink wine," she said finally. "But I don't like drinking around Jeremy. I'm trying to set a good example."

I nodded. "I understand."

"You see," she said, and paused to swallow, "Wesley was an alcoholic."

An alcoholic who owned three bars? Ay, yi yi!

"I'm sorry," I said. "Never mind the wine. I can bring the tea kettle, if you'd like."

She managed a smile. "Thanks. I would like that."

I met Tony's gaze. He gave a little nod of approval.

I finished my salad before eating my second piece of pizza. As I picked it up, I saw the two cowboys—our trail guide and his buddy—take seats at the next table.

Ted. That was the trail guide's name. He sat with his back toward us.

The other one had been out sick that morning. He looked fine now, as he tucked into a large plate of spaghetti.

Could Ted, or his partner, be the killer?

No, I thought. Awfully ballsy to hang a guy and then lead a trail ride within fifty yards of the body.

Unless that was a bold strategy for appearing innocent.

I took a swallow of mocha, feeling like I wasn't very good at this detective stuff. I seemed to get mired in a welter of conflicting conjecture. How did Tony manage it?

"I'd better get back," Lisette said. She had finished her single slice of pizza and small salad. "I need to get some dinner for Jeremy," she added as she stood and picked up her plate and mug.

"I'll come with you," I said, and stuffed the last bite of my pizza into my mouth.

Tony remained, placidly finishing his meal while we turned in our dishes. Lisette returned to the food line, which was short now, and asked for takeout pizza for Jeremy. I glanced at the dessert—a platter of cookies, each large enough to choke a horse. Too sweet, I decided, but maybe Jeremy would like one. I suggested this to Lisette, who agreed and added a cookie wrapped in a paper towel to her takeout. We returned to the dining hall, where Tony was just rising from the table.

"I'll walk you back," he said, picking up his plate.

We bundled up and headed out with our burdens. I paused at the Ghost House to collect the tea things and mugs, stuffing them all into a canvas bag. Lisette and Tony were waiting by the cottonwood trees, and as I rejoined them I glanced up into the branches, listening. All I heard was the sighing of the wind.

We headed up the hill to Lisette's casita. "I'm gonna check on the game," Tony told us at the door. "Text me when you want to leave, and I'll come walk you back," he added to me.

The offer wasn't necessary, but it was kind. He was keeping an eye out for me as well as for Lisette. He kissed my frozen cheek, his breath warm, his smell enticing.

Lisette opened the door. The casita was silent. She and I went in, setting our burdens on the coffee table. With a wave, Tony pulled the door shut.

I unpacked my canvas bag and found a plug for my travel kettle while Lisette went through the door into the next room. Her voice, speaking softly, and Jeremy's groggy response reached me from the depths of the casita. I filled the kettle and set it to boil, then set up the teapot with some peppermint teabags I had nabbed from the dining hall. Lisette would need to sleep well that night.

As the kettle boiled, Lisette and Jeremy came in. Jeremy looked tired and sad, but brightened at the sight of the pizza. I set the tea brewing, then joined them in the sitting room.

"Hi, Jeremy," I said. "I'm Ellen, remember?"

He nodded, mouth full of pizza.

"Guess what?" I said. "It's snowing! Do you get much snow in Houston?"

Jeremy shook his head, eyes wide, then looked toward the window.

"We'll look at it after you've eaten," Lisette said.

Jeremy swallowed. "Is there enough to make a snowman?"

"There might be by morning," I said.

Jeremy looked at his mother with a blinding smile, then went back to the pizza.

Wow, I thought. What a great kid.

No way could he have killed his dad. No way.

I hated to think it, but there might have been times when he *wished* he could kill Wesley, or just stop Wesley. But this boy was too sweet, I thought, to actually commit such a crime.

Not to mention the impossibility of his hoisting Wesley into a tree. Even together, he and his mother wouldn't have the strength to hang that man, much less subdue him. Not that I considered either of them a likely suspect.

My timer went off, and I poured tea for Lisette and myself. We drank, chatting about the weather in Houston and in New Mexico. Jeremy asked shyly if it snowed in Santa Fe. I told him it did, and asked if he'd ever seen *farolitos.*

"Faro-what?"

"*Farolitos.* Some people call them *luminarias.* They're paper bags, like a lunch bag, with a bit of sand in the bottom and a candle."

"Oh! Luminaries!"

Ugh. "Yes," I said, smiling.

"We have those. But they're plastic, not paper."

I explained the tradition, and described how streets all over Santa Fe were lit with *farolitos* on Christmas Eve. Jeremy turned to his mother, excited.

"Can we go to Santa Fe next Christmas?"

"Maybe," Lisette said. "We'll see."

Jeremy was so excited about the snow that he actually postponed devouring his giant cookie in favor of going outside. His mother gave permission as long as he bundled up first, so we all put on our coats and hats and stepped out into the snow, which was about three inches deep now.

Good thing Tony and I hadn't tried to drive to the Abiquiu Inn. Getting back in this would have been Not Fun.

We stayed in the arc of the casita's porch light. Jeremy played with the snow, running it through his gloved fingers, then trying to make a snowball. It was too dry and powdery, and fell apart in his hands. In the morning it might be better, when things were a little warmer.

I wondered how the football game was going. Had Tony picked up any clues? Had he been sucked into watching the game? God, I hoped he wasn't a big-time fan. The prospect of being a cop's wife was bad enough without the added risk of becoming a football widow.

Well, there was always tea.

My thoughts drifted to the murder. Plenty of people had a casual interest in shutting Wesley up, but did any of them really have the nerve, the means, and the opportunity to kill him? Lisette (and Jeremy) had the strongest motive, but the least likely means. Jeremy, at least, had an alibi. And I was certain, just from their personalities and their behavior, that they were both innocent.

Who, then, had killed Wesley? Could Tony's speculation that it was a hit job be right?

Except what professional assassin would stage a murder out in the boonies, and bludgeon the victim and shoot him full of buckshot before stringing him up? If it was a hit, it was a very odd one.

There was one factor I'd left out, I realized as I watched Jeremy play. Hate crime.

A crime that made no sense, at least to me. Maybe Wesley had been killed, not because he was obnoxious, but simply because he was black.

I looked at Lisette, her face soft as she watched her son. If the murder was strictly a hate crime, then they were both at risk. Which was why Tony and Deputy Trujillo were being watchful.

And the killer could be anyone. Anyone at all. How could we know which of the guests, or the staff, at Ghost Ranch carried that kind of hate in their hearts?

And to top it all off, I realized, the Roans were Texans.

New Mexico and Texas had hated each other for centuries. I had grown up with Texas jokes, thinking they were normal. It wasn't until I went away to college that I realized that not everyone in the country told Texas jokes. And what expressed itself in jokes nowadays had been open warfare not so very long ago. In Captain Dusenberry's time, Texans had invaded New Mexico. Even now, every few decades, some nutjob organization— usually extremist and heavily armed, but fortunately small in number—tried to claim that New Mexico belonged to Texas.

Texans, black and female (in Lisette's case) or underage (in Jeremy's). Unfamiliar with New Mexico's culture and customs. The deck was seriously stacked against them.

Movement to the side made me turn and peer toward the parking lot. A solitary figure was approaching. I watched, ready to shout an alarm, until I recognized Tony's shape. He joined me and stood watching Jeremy, who was making a design in the snow with his footprints. Lisette glanced at him and he gave her a smile.

"How's the game going?" I asked.

Tony shrugged. "Nothing special. Texans are getting whomped."

"Oh, boy."

Lisette did not react to this news. She seemed to be as uninterested in football as I was.

Jeremy came up to us, breathless and glowing. "Hi, Mr. Aragón! Will you help me make a snowman?"

Tony brushed at the snow with a foot. "Not with this stuff. It's too dry. But you could make a snow angel. Ever done that?"

Jeremy shook his head.

"I'll show you."

So Lisette and I watched Tony and Jeremy lie down in the snow, sweeping it with their arms and legs. Following Tony's lead, Jeremy hopped up, peered at his handiwork, and laughed with delight, then found a fresh spot and flopped down in it to make another.

Tony joined me, brushing snow from his arms and legs. I helped, brushing off his back. He grinned at me. "Haven't done that in a long time."

"That's enough for now," Lisette called as Jeremy got up again and began to range farther from the light to find fresh snow. "You can do some more in the morning." She brushed down her son, then led us all inside, where I put the kettle on again. My toes and fingers were chilled, and I hadn't even been playing with the snow.

I shed my coat and draped it over the desk chair. Jeremy pelted Tony with questions about how to make a snowman.

"I need a carrot, and coal for the eyes, right? Where do I get coal?"

"It doesn't have to be coal, Tony said. "You can use rocks, or prunes."

"Prunes?" I said.

"Yeah, *Abuela* used to give us prunes to use. Old ones that had dried out."

Lisette and I both laughed. Jeremy asked, very seriously,

where he could get prunes.

"And I need a scarf, right? A scarf and a hat? And mittens?"

"Not necessarily," Tony said. "You can keep it simple. Couple of sticks for arms."

"Or you can get creative," I told Jeremy. "Maybe tomorrow morning you can go on a scavenger hunt for what you need. I bet the kitchen staff would give you a carrot."

"Yeah!" Jeremy said, eyes wide with enthusiasm. He headed for the desk. "I gotta make a list!"

Lisette intercepted him as he was about to go for her art supplies. Instead she gave him the notepad and a pen, and sat him in the armchair, murmuring softly. Tony, who had flopped on the sofa, watched with a bemused expression.

The kettle boiled and I made peppermint tea for Tony and Jeremy. Jeremy, absorbed in his list, complained that he wanted cocoa, then subsided as his mother spoke softly to him again.

"Thank you," she said, joining me on the couch. "He hasn't smiled like that in I don't know how long."

"If you need help in the morning, let me know. We were going to leave after breakfast—" I glanced at Tony, who didn't quite shake his head, but tilted it. "—but I think we'll end up waiting for the roads to be cleared."

"Thanks," Lisette said.

A few minutes later, Jeremy started to fidget in his chair. He tore his list off the pad, doodled on the next page, then tore off that page and balled it up, throwing it with unnecessary force at a nearby wastebasket, and missing.

He's remembered.

"Well, we ought to go," I said, standing. I collected my tea gear and packed it back into the canvas bag.

"Thank you," Lisette said softly, adding Jeremy's mug. "This has been a big help."

I gave her a hug. "I'm glad. See you in the morning. Call us if you need anything."

She smiled at me. A brave smile, less strained than before. She still had a hard road ahead, but for now, things were peaceful, at least.

Tony and I made our farewells and headed back to the Ghost House. Snow still falling, a bit heavier now. The ranch was quiet. Very few footprints in the snow. People were holed up inside, waiting for morning.

I wondered how much Jeremy knew about his father's death. Not much, I hoped. No details. Bad enough that it was a murder investigation, which he surely knew.

Our casita was warm and dark. Tony stepped in ahead of me to turn on a light and look around. Cop habit: check for bad guys. He shrugged out of his coat and tossed it on the dresser, then went into the bathroom.

I hung my coat on a chair, then put my tea things back on their improvised table, ready for morning. Turned on the bedside lamp and turned off the brighter overhead. It was time to get cozy. I put on my pajamas, grateful for the warmth of winter flannel. Collecting my book, I slid into bed and propped myself up on the pillows.

Tony finished his evening ablutions and emerged in pajama bottoms, no top. I hopped up to brush my teeth. As I passed him, he caught me in a hug and held me for a while. I relaxed, hugging back. It had been a rough day.

When I came back to bed, Tony was propped on his pillows, hands behind his head, frowning at the ceiling. I slid between the sheets and curled up against him.

"It's late," I said softly. "Let it go."

He looked at me and sighed. "Just thinking."

I stroked his hair. "You were very kind to Jeremy."

"Kid lost his dad," Tony said, and swallowed.

Oh, God. I hadn't thought of that. Of course this would bring up old feelings for Tony.

I hugged him. He rolled over and kissed me hungrily.

We forgot to turn off the light.

11

IT WAS DARK, AND I WAS SAWING A TREE BRANCH, trying to drop it before the man hanging from it died of strangulation. "Zzzt, zzzt," went the saw. "Zzzt, zzzt." Almost through the branch, but it might be too late. The hanged man wasn't moving.

"Zzzt, zzzt."

Tony sat up, and I startled awake. His phone lit up the room, blinding me.

That's what I'd heard. Tony's muted phone, buzzing against the table top. Sighing, I closed my eyes against the glare as tension drained from me.

"It's Trujillo," Tony said. "The M.E.'s report came in."

He threw back the covers and stood. Cringing, I curled up in the blankets. "You're going now?"

"Yeah. I'll meet you at breakfast."

From the refuge of the bed, I listened to him dress. He leaned over to kiss me, then was gone, pulling the door firmly shut behind him.

M.E. Military Educator. Meat and Eggs. Middle Earth.

Oh. Medical Examiner.

They must have taken the body away yesterday, before the snow started. Which meant the Medical Examiner had worked into the night, probably, to finish the autopsy.

With speculations about the condition of the deceased revolving in my brain, further sleep was unlikely. I arose, despite the darkness, and nudged the thermostat up a notch, then took a long, hot shower. I sighed at the sight of the pretty dress I'd brought for our dinner at the Inn, still hanging on the back of the door. I should just pack it away, I thought as I put on my last set of clean jeans and shirt. Then I pulled on my sweater and made tea.

It was still dark out. Ignoring the chill, I pushed aside the curtains in the Room of Many Chairs and sat watching the coming dawn. It was still snowing, although half-heartedly, as if the clouds were getting tired. I made myself as comfortable as possible in the modest chair, drank my tea, and thought back over the previous day's events.

I'd found another body. Kris and Julio would be merciless, but with luck I'd keep the story from spreading all over Santa Fe. Maybe I'd neglect to tell Gina.

Actually, I had been pretty lucky, except for my annoying interview with Sheriff Romero. Deputy Trujillo had been meticulously polite and respectful, perhaps because of my connection with Tony. They were of a generation: colleagues, simpatico. And because of this, and because of my engagement, professional courtesy had been extended to me. An interesting sensation.

My mug was empty. I got up for more tea, and returned to my vigil, watching for the first lightening of the sky. What would this day bring? Tony's last day off—and he was up to his neck in someone else's investigation. And, apparently, enjoying it.

Quite possibly, I would never figure out what made Tony tick. Was he driven by grief? I didn't think so. More like he wanted to carry on his father's mission. He took the motto "serve and protect" to heart, more than most cops I'd encountered. Granted, I had been lucky enough not to encounter that many. But the news was full of complaints about police brutality, of bully culture and mistreatment of the vulnerable. I had never seen any indication that Tony was capable of that.

Finally the blackness shifted to dark gray, and shapes began to take form outside the window. The cottonwoods were looming shadows, bark painted in snow. Flakes were still falling. As I stood to replenish my tea, I could see the trench Tony had made in the fallen snow on his way down to the welcome center. It looked knee-deep.

"Holy Moly!"

I might not get home today.

I found my phone. Just past 7:00. I didn't want to disturb Nat, but I'd have to tell her to be ready to stand in for me at the tearoom tomorrow. Likewise, I should give Kris a heads-up. And Julio, probably.

But it could wait until after breakfast. Which started at 7:30. Considering the snow, it would be a good idea to leave a little early.

I cleaned up my tea things, then put on my hiking boots and bundled up. Scarf, hat, gloves, and the winter coat. Making sure I had my phone in my purse, I headed out.

The sky was now a uniform pale gray. Tiny snowflakes continued to fall in a desultory way. The snow was just over my knees, maybe eighteen inches deep. Other than the marks of Tony's passage, I saw no disturbance, and I had to blaze my own way when I turned toward the dining hall. The road had not been plowed. Fortunately, the snow was still powdery, so it wasn't hard to push my way through it.

Not until I was close to the dining hall did I see the marks of other travelers. Several trails came across the field from the direction of the Staff House. Maybe the kitchen staff, as well as others?

Great deduction, Inspector Rosings.

Clearly I was in need of sustenance.

The cafeteria line was bright and cheery and steamy. Pancakes and oatmeal were offered in addition to cold cereal and fruit. I chose pancakes, but the only syrup offered was pancake syrup, and I preferred real maple. Disappointed, I picked up some butter, then in a stroke of inspiration, collected some packets of raspberry jam from the condiments table to adorn the pancakes. Very European.

I looked around for Lisette or Tony, and saw neither. Stopping briefly for coffee, I made my way toward the fireplace, where the morning's fire was crackling as if it had just been coaxed to life.

Most of the guests who were present had collected near the fire. I took note of Flag Hat, sans the cap for once, and a couple of his buddies, with large stacks of pancakes and bacon on their plates. Several recognizable guests from either the trail ride or the O'Keeffe house tour were present, and I spotted Ted's partner —I never had caught his name—at a table near the windows.

Choosing a seat at the first unpopulated table away from the fire allowed me to keep all of these people in view. I made myself comfortable, drank some coffee, then took out my phone and texted Tony:

> I'm in the dining hall. Flag
> Hat is here.

No immediate answer, so I put the phone down and proceeded to enjoy my pancakes. On this chilly morning, they were a delight. I kept an eye out for Lisette as best I could, but my back was to the entrance. I hoped she'd notice me and join me when she arrived.

I finished my coffee and debated whether to get a second cup or some milk to accompany the rest of my pancakes. My phone buzzed with a text:

> Be there in a few.

Milk, I decided. I fetched myself a glass, scanning the room for Lisette and Jeremy, then returned to my seat. A moment later, Ted strolled by, headed for the table where his partner was sitting. He paused beside me.

"All alone this morning?"

I shot him a "seriously?" look, and replied, "My fiancé is on his way."

"Oh. Well, have a nice day, ma'am."

He ambled away, leaving me annoyed. Maybe it was the disregard of professional distance, which I expected from someone I'd hired to perform a service. Maybe it was the suggestion of flirtation in his manner—also inappropriate for a professional. Or maybe I was still annoyed that I hadn't been able to hear his narration on the tour. He rubbed me the wrong way, that was certain.

I finished my breakfast, drained my milk, and considered refilling my coffee after all, just as an excuse to remain. Flag Hat and his friends were being slightly loud, but no raucous arguments broke out. I searched the faces of the others I had recognized, looking for furtive or unusual behavior, but everyone was acting tediously normal. The woman whose horse had tried to bolt on the trail ride was fretting about her flight home the next day, worried she wouldn't be able to drive her rental car to Albuquerque. That was as unusual as it got.

Still no Tony. He'd probably been unable to tear himself away from the MI's report. I turned in my tray, refilled my coffee, and strolled toward the windows, looking out at the snow. The sky was a bit brighter, a hopeful sign that the storm was coming to an end.

"Seen Ezra?" said a voice off to the side. It was Ted, the trail guide. I sidled a bit in that direction.

"Nah. Bet he's holed up in his cabin." The other cowboy. "What're we going to do today?"

"Clean tack."

"What about the bay?"

"I'll deal with him."

What about the bay? I wondered. That big bay that had been saddled and waiting for the rider who would never come: Wesley Roan. I presumed that was what they were talking about, but they suddenly lowered their voices. Maybe they'd noticed me by the window.

Wesley had been dragged behind a horse, I recalled.

I finished my coffee and strolled away. Lisette and a sleepy-looking Jeremy emerged from the cafeteria line, and I went to greet them.

"Good morning!" I said, smiling.

Lisette smiled back, briefly. The shades were back. "Morning," she said. "We slept in."

"Good day for it. How do you like the snow, Jeremy?"

"It's OK," he mumbled.

"Let's find a table," Lisette said.

"Can we sit by the fire?" Jeremy said plaintively.

She nodded, and glanced at me. "You've eaten," she said.

"Yes. I think I'll get a little more coffee."

"Come and sit with us."

She led Jeremy toward the fireplace. I fixed myself another improvised mocha and joined them, this time sitting with my back to the fire. Taking a sip, I watched Jeremy pick at his pancakes, then take a slice of bacon off of a stack on the side of his plate. Lisette poured milk onto a small bowl of oatmeal with granola sprinkled on top.

"I hope you slept all right," I said.

Lisette shrugged, and looked at Jeremy. "We got some sleep."

I watched them try to eat, not bothering them with any more conversation. They were in shock, still. They needed time and rest to recover.

Feeling I was watched, I looked up. Flag Hat Guy was staring at us, or maybe at the Roans. As I looked at him his gaze shifted to me, and for a second I saw sullen resentment in his eyes, then his expression changed to confusion. He looked down at his plate, picked up a piece of bacon, and stuffed it in his mouth in two bites.

Refusing to be rattled, I watched him a bit longer. He did not look up again. My attention was finally drawn away by the welcome sight of Tony, cafeteria tray in hand, scanning the room until he saw me and started forward.

"Morning," he said as he sat beside me. "Hi, Jeremy."

Jeremy gave him a shy glance. "Hi."

Tony picked up his mug and took a swig of coffee, watching the Roans. Their lack of conversation didn't bother him at all. He ate pancakes and drank coffee in comfortable silence, and I noticed Jeremy relaxing a bit in his presence.

Catching Tony's eye, I lifted my chin toward where Flag Hat was sitting. Tony acknowledged this with a slight nod.

By the time Tony finished his pancakes, Lisette had finished her oatmeal. Jeremy had eaten all his bacon and was turning his remaining pancakes into mush with the back of his fork.

"Time to go," said Lisette.

"Plans for the day?" I asked.

"I have to make…arrangements," she said.

I nodded. We all got up and disposed of our dishes, then put on our coats and went out into the snow.

The storm had stopped, the sky was brighter, and people were trudging through the snowdrifts here and there. An engine's roar preceded the sound of a jacked up dualie pickup with a plow blade, scraping snow from the road. A couple of the pedestrians cheered as it went by, throwing up a fan of snow to one side.

We made our way back, following our own tracks from earlier, which had begun to pack down the snow into a reasonable trail. Tony and I parted from the Roans at the Ghost House, Lisette declining Tony's offer to escort them to their casita. She dropped an arm around Jeremy's shoulders as they started up the hill. We watched until they were out of sight, then went in.

"Deputy Trujillo was at work early," I commented.

"He spent the night," Tony said. "Crashed in a dorm room."

"Ah."

"Want to hear about the autopsy? It's interesting."

Did I *want* to hear about it? Not really, but I'd promised Tony my support. If I was destined to be his sounding board, I might as well get used to it.

"Sure," I said.

Tony hopped onto the bed and stretched out, inviting me to join him. I took off my boots first, then snuggled beside him. So nice to just cuddle.

"Roan didn't die from being hanged," Tony said.

"What?"

"He was already dead when he was strung up."

I sat up. "But...."

"He didn't die from being dragged either. That happened after he died."

I met Tony's gaze. He was enjoying himself. "And he didn't die from being shot, I assume?"

"Nope. One round of buckshot, fired at a distance. Would have stung like hell if he'd been alive, but he wasn't."

I frowned. "Then what killed him?"

Tony smiled. "The blow to the head. And what's interesting is, the blow itself only gave him a nasty gash. But apparently it rocked his head back so hard, it broke his neck."

I blinked. "So his neck *was* broken, but not by the rope?"

"Right."

"Did he—die instantly?"

"Pretty quick, yeah."

"Then why bother with the rest? The shotgun, the hanging?"

"Good question."

I sighed, and snuggled back into Tony's armpit. "Spite," I said. "Or hate."

"Two slightly different views of the same motive."

Tony had on the sweater that Nat and Manny had given him for Christmas, I realized. How had I not noticed it before? Too preoccupied with the Roans and their troubles. I needed to regain my equanimity.

And yet, there was an unsolved murder. Tony wanted my feedback. And if I could help the Roans in any way, I must.

I stroked the sweater over his chest, following the narrow stripe with a fingertip. "What was he hit with?"

"Another good question. We don't know. Something hard, with an edge, but not sharpened."

"Like a board?"

"Probably heavier than that. It—um—did significant damage."

"And the killer didn't leave it at the scene."

"Well, the crime scene we found was not the murder scene."

"Oh. But the—criminal—took the trouble of covering their tracks."

"Yeah."

"So what crime happened there?" I asked, because I was getting puzzled.

"Tampering with evidence. And a hate crime, possibly."

"Possibly. Depending on...?"

"There were no messages of hate. Usually a hate crime is defined either by overt hate messages, or by context."

"And context in this case..."

"Is unclear."

I thought over the past couple of days. "I think it's fair to say Wesley Roan was hated."

Tony stroked my hair. "Is it? Or was he just disliked because he was incredibly annoying?"

"If you had seen the way Flag Hat looked at us this morning...he wasn't just annoyed."

"Was he looking at you, or the Roans?"

"I'm not sure. But when I looked back, he looked away."

"Where was this?"

"In the dining hall. Before you got there."

Tony's eyes narrowed as he frowned. Had Flag Hat been present, he might have trembled in his designer boots.

"Anything else interesting?" I asked, to distract him.

"Yeah. The angle of the buckshot indicated the shooter was above Roan. Well above him, like at least ten feet."

"So...?"

"So maybe they were above the arroyo."

"Or in the tree," I said. "But not on the ground."

Tony gave a huff of laughter. "Yeah. Why climb up in a tree to shoot, when you could shoot from the ground? But the angles are all wrong."

"Why is the big question," I said. "Why did Wesley run out to that arroyo? Why did the killer shoot him after he was dead, and drag him to a tree and string him up?"

"Well, stringing him up is pretty obvious."

"Is it? You just said that context matters. What if hate had nothing to do with this?"

Tony leaned his head back to look at me. "What's your motive, then?"

"Maybe someone was after his money. You'll need to check out his will—"

"That's underway," Tony said.

I paused, mixed feelings hitting me on the subject of Wesley's will. On the one hand, I hoped every penny he had went to Lisette. On the other, that would add to her motivation for killing her husband. Or having him killed.

Neither of which I truly believed was possible.

"Or maybe," I said slowly, groping after a new thought, "a competitor of his wanted him out of the way."

Tony raised an eyebrow. "Battle of the Houston sports bars?"

"Territorialism. Ancient and honorable reason for killing your neighbor."

"Well, I don't know about honorable."

"Or maybe Wesley was trying to blackmail someone," I said.

"Why would he do that?"

"It's the sort of thing assholes do."

"Not all assholes."

I had to chuckle at that. Tony rolled on his side and pulled me closer.

"We're getting into extreme speculation here," he said.

"I thought speculation was the name of the game."

"Mm. We could play another game."

He ran a hand along my shoulder blades, setting them tingling. My brain sent some happy affirmative signals shooting through me.

"What game do you have in mind?" I asked, and nipped his chin.

His answer was non-verbal.

Some time later, after we'd showered and dressed, we headed for the welcome center to confer with Deputy Trujillo, who had been sending Tony texts for half an hour. I sent a thought of gratitude toward my mother, who had taught me always to pack extra socks and underwear.

Outside, the sun was gleaming through the overcast, a pale ball in a gray sky. The air was a little warmer It was still bitter cold, so there hadn't been much melt-off yet. Our footsteps scrunched as we made our way to the road, where the snow was packed by the passing of the plow truck and other vehicles.

We could get out, hurrah! Home tonight!

That is, if I could get the Camry onto the road. And if Tony could tear himself away from the case. I glanced at him sidelong. His mood was cheerful, which I found interesting, as that wasn't how he usually reacted to a murder case.

But then, it wasn't *his* case. He was on vacation, technically. He had just chosen to help out Deputy Trujillo. Maybe he was having fun with the problem-solving, without feeling the usual pressure of responsibility.

"You up for a hike?" Tony asked, his breath fogging.

"Now? In the snow?"

"Yeah—mostly walking. Not on ridges like the Matrimonial Trail. But it might be kind of long."

"Oh, well. In that case, why not?"

I was being flippant, but I got the impression Tony wasn't joking. Why he suddenly wanted to hike, I had no idea—but I was curious. It must have something to do with the case.

We reached the welcome center just as Deputy Trujillo was emerging. He wore a sheepskin coat over his khaki uniform, and the Stetson hat he'd had on the night before.

"There you are," he said to Tony. "Almost gave up."

"Sorry for the delay," Tony said.

"It's OK. My uncle just got here. You need to go in?" He gestured toward the center.

Tony shook his head. I dug my gloved hands into my pockets, wondering if I'd regret agreeing to hike, because I now suspected what our destination would be.

The center's door opened and a tall man in a sheepskin coat over jeans stepped out. He wore no hat; his long, black hair was braided and tied with a single feather; and he was Bernardo Milagro.

I'm sure my eyes were like saucers. In the daylight, I could see threads of silver running through his hair, and deep creases at the corners of his eyes. He had a well-worn leather satchel slung over his shoulder, and carried a flute in one hand. He squinted at the bright spot in the sky that was the sun, then looked at me and Tony and grinned.

"It's the bride and groom. Morning!"

"Morning," I said, not quite sure I wasn't dreaming.

Milagro looked at Trujillo. "Let's do this."

Trujillo nodded, head down, and suddenly I recognized the movement. I *had* seen him before. On the stage, backing up Milagro on the electric piano. My impression of his personality underwent a rapid and radical transformation.

Trujillo led the way along the trail that led to the stables. A faint hope that we were going to ride was smacked down by my sensible side. Riding in snow would be dangerous for horses and riders alike, even if the ranch management had no objections, which they surely would. Liability, etc., etc. Not to mention fatiguing the animals.

We walked past the corrals, where said animals were out of sight, probably in their stalls munching hay. Trujillo led us to the horse trail and along it. There were no prints of any kind on it, but the indentation in the snow marked the path that the horses' hooves had worn across the mesas. The snow wasn't as deep there as it was where there was foliage. We walked single file, Trujillo in the lead, followed by Milagro, then me, with Tony again bringing up the rear. No one talked.

Knowing this would be a long walk, I tried to occupy myself by thinking about things I needed to do for the tearoom. We had February reservations coming in already. Kris wanted to extend our hours, as we'd done in December, but I wasn't sure I was ready to do that again so soon. It would mean more hours for my staff, or hiring additional help. There was also the special Valentine's Day event I had tentatively planned. That would need to be firmed up and I'd have to reach an agreement with the musicians...

Somewhere in the midst of considering these and other details, I found myself going over the murder case again. The tearoom slid from my thoughts, replaced by the image—burned into my memory—of Wesley Roan's body swinging gently from a cottonwood.

Why had the killer been so unnecessarily thorough? Why

bludgeon a man to death, then follow it up with shooting him, dragging him, and hanging him? That spoke of intense animosity.

A large bird flew by overhead and I paused to watch it. It was black: crow or raven, I wasn't sure. Because we were in O'Keeffe's country, I immediately thought of *Black Bird,* another of my mom's posters. Tony came up beside me and gave my shoulder a squeeze.

"You OK?" he said softly.

I nodded and turned to catch up to the others.

Walking behind Milagro, I had leisure to admire his braid—which was very thick—and the feather, which was tied in with strips of leather and beadwork that glinted even in the filtered sunlight. They reminded me of the dragonfly necklace he had given me and Tony. His satchel was plain, heavy leather that had been well-cared-for over years of use. It made me think of the pouch I had found: Captain Dusenberry's treasure.

Milagro's flute was a thing of beauty: dark wood, carved and polished, ornamented with beads and a bear fetish made of bright turquoise that was lashed to the flute with deerskin. He'd made it himself, I was sure. I remembered hearing he made all his own flutes, and there had been one for sale on his table. This might be one of the ones he had played at the concert.

I was hiking in the snow with Bernardo Milagro. The day was getting surreal.

I was no longer cold at all, I realized. I was a little concerned about being out here without water, but there was plenty of snow if we got thirsty, and the sky was gradually brightening, so cold wasn't going to be an immediate danger. I looked at the cliffs, trying to gauge how far we'd come. We had not yet passed O'Keeffe's ranch house.

Even as I thought this, I saw the roughly horizontal lines of the rail fence ahead, covered with snow. The fence slanted haphazardly; the windows were dark, empty eyes. It truly looked abandoned now. We passed by and headed on toward the cliffs. As we climbed a shallow slope, I could see the impression in the snow of the service road that ran past the ranch house, where the landscape tour bus would normally run. All of today's tours had been canceled—because of the snow, not to mention the murder—but would the plow be coming along this road? Would it destroy unseen evidence?

For that matter, if there were tracks beneath the snow, would there be anything left of them when it melted? I didn't know.

We made our way down a steep cut into an arroyo, then switchbacked up the other side. There'd been several such crossings on the trail ride, I remembered. We were getting farther from the ranch complex, closer to the cliffs. They seemed to loom over us now, towers touching the pearly sky.

My feet were beginning to ache, and my legs were getting tired from walking in heavy boots (though I was grateful for them, because they kept my feet warm). To distract myself, I looked at the cliffs and thought about O'Keeffe's many paintings of this land. These were the red hills she so loved. I wondered if they had inspired *White Shell with Red*. The background in that painting was the same bright, vermilion-red of these sandstone hills.

I hoped Lisette would return to her art. I hoped seeing O'Keeffe's places had inspired her, and that her art would help her through her grief. Maybe the trip would inspire Jeremy, too. Certainly it was good for him to see places like this.

For Wesley, it had been too late. He was too ingrained in his football culture and in his own life habits to be touched by natural beauty. And he'd had plenty of company. I wondered why Flag Hat and the other football fans were here at all. Had all of them been dragged unwilling to Ghost Ranch by family members who were seeking inspiration?

That couldn't be the case. They must be here for better reasons than that. What would bring a man like Flag Hat Guy here? A workshop or retreat? Maybe he was actually a paleontologist who just happened to love football?

Tony might know, if Trujillo had shared his interviews. Not that I was curious to know myself.

I looked up from watching where I placed my feet in the partially-trodden snow, to where Trujillo was blazing the trail for us. He'd called Milagro his uncle. So he *was* Pueblo, or part Pueblo. And he'd been at the concert. A musician, as well as a cop. I remembered Tony's guitar, and how surprised and delighted I'd been when he played it and sang for me.

Below the cliffs, a tall, barren bush rose at the edge of the mesa. As I looked at it more closely, I realized it was a tree: the top of a cottonwood growing in an arroyo. I glanced at Trujillo, still breaking through the snow in the trail, its indentation winding away before him, snake-like, across the snowy mesa. This was looking familiar. I looked at the cliffs, and westward at the more distant horizon, also defined by cliffs, with blue mountains marching away to the southwest. The tempo of my pulse increased a notch.

Glancing southward, I looked for the ranch road. There it was, a wide and shallow dip in the snow, curving northward. Beyond it, the sagebrush was beginning to emerge from its blanket of snow. The hollow darkness between branches showed black, like little caves, and I wondered if little animals were hiding in some of them, waiting for the sun's return.

The day was getting warmer. Our breath no longer froze in the air. Ahead, Trujillo halted, then Milagro stopped beside him. I stayed back, waiting. Tony stepped up even with me.

We stood at the edge of a descent into the arroyo. The deep-worn trail rang more bells of familiarity. Looking northward, I saw a bit more of the tree that was not a bush.

Wesley's tree.

My stomach was suddenly heavy, trying to drop out of me. I swallowed, realizing my throat was dry. A sip of water would have been good. I wasn't yet desperate enough to eat snow.

The two men in front of me exchanged a murmured word, then Trujillo started northward along the top edge of the arroyo, going more slowly as he left the trail. Again, we followed single file in his tracks. He avoided the small bumps in the snowy ground that were clumps of wild grass or baby trees, and skirted the larger bushes, junipers, and the occasional cholla. I wondered nervously if there was prickly pear beneath the snow, then reminded myself that even if I had the bad luck to step on a hidden cactus, my boots should protect me.

The cottonwood tree loomed as we got closer, bare branches reaching skyward. It was bigger than I'd thought, its crown rising a good fifteen feet or more above the edge of the mesa. When we'd come as close to it as we could without descending into the arroyo, we stopped again.

Milagro stepped forward, joining Trujillo at the edge. Glancing back, he motioned to me and Tony to join them. I moved to Milagro's right, and Tony stepped to my right.

We all stood staring silently at the tree. I gazed down through the upper branches, unwillingly trying to discern which bough was the one on which Wesley had been hanged. A low one that grew out over the arroyo, I remembered.

Milagro reached into his satchel and withdrew a gourd rattle. Suddenly he began to sing, the first syllable a bark that made me jump, sharp in the cold desert air. It was Tiwa, so I had no hope of understanding the words, but the meaning was crystal clear. He sang with the anguish of one who has lost a brother. After a few lines, he began to shake the rattle, slowly, in the rhythm of a heartbeat.

That rhythm evoked every feast-day dance I'd ever been to. My feet wanted to move with it: right LEFT, right LEFT, right LEFT. Shadows of the deer dancers, the buffalo dancers, the butterfly dancers and corn dancers stepped through my memories.

Was this a sing?

Still playing the rhythm as he sang, Milagro held the rattle out toward Trujillo, who took it without missing a beat. A few more phrases, then Milagro raised the flute while the rattle's heartbeat continued.

If the singing had sounded mournful, the flute was doubly so. I realized I was holding my shoulders tensely, and deliberately relaxed them. As I let go, the flute's sorrow flowed through me. Tears filled my eyes and overflowed. Tears for a wrongful death, for a joyless life, for the pain of a wounded family, now broken.

The music went on and on. At times Trujillo shook the rattle in a continuous buzz, and memory played a drumroll along with it while he joined Milagro in singing: a calling, a summoning. Then the rhythm would begin again, and another song—another dance —would follow.

Finally I had no more tears. I swallowed, trying to be silent, trying not to sniff. Once I raised my hand to wipe my face. In the cold, the tears chilled my cheeks even more.

Milagro sang again, played the flute again. Cold crept up my legs now that we were standing still. To keep my feet from falling asleep, I eased my weight gently back and forth with the rhythm of the rattle: right *left*, right *left*, right *left*.

Another roll of the rattle, another chanting call, and then three strong beats, followed by silence. I held still, listening to the echo of the rhythm and the song. A breeze stirred the tree branches, rattling them together. Their motion drew my eye, and through them I saw a splash of blue and white.

Tony's hand slid into mine. I turned my head to meet his gaze. His eyes were dark and intense. The music had called something out of him, just as it had with me. There was fierce feeling in his gaze, but it wasn't anger. It was love—fierce love—as though his soul was saying "no matter what the world throws our way, I will be here for you."

I drew a deep and slightly shaky breath, and let it out in a sigh. Trujillo held out the silent rattle to his uncle, who stowed it in the satchel.

That blue and white troubled me. They were not colors that fit into the landscape, even with the snow. Wanting to know what it was, I took a couple of steps to the right, trying to find a gap in the branches to see through. Tony came with me, steadying me as I groped for level footing. Some of the branches did not look right, until they suddenly resolved into fence posts. Even more haphazard than the O'Keeffe homestead fence, these posts were barely kept upright by long-neglected barbed wire. In a couple of places they were down, the wire hidden by the snow. The blue was a sign, roughly lettered in white: KEEP OUT, then a little smaller, DANGER UNSTABLE, followed by rows of text decreasing in size. I remembered another such sign, seen on the trail ride, not so very far from where we stood.

How sad that someone was so frightened as to think such signs were needful. How sad that sometimes, they were. I looked at it again, and noticed now that the sign and the fence didn't just flank the arroyo: they crossed it.

What I had thought to be a bend in the arroyo, curving around the cottonwood tree, was in fact the end of the arroyo—or rather, its beginning. A short distance beyond the crazy fence, a jumble of yellow boulders tumbled into the bottom, blocking the way. A wash, coming down out of the hills, that only became a seasonal stream bed when it reached the softer sandstone mesa. Snow-capped, the rocks looked smaller than they really were.

Now I understood the sign, and I understood something more. In the dark, the pale arroyo would have appeared to lead straight into that fence. Could Wesley have stumbled into it, or even across it?

But there was the sign. He must have seen that, even if he didn't have a flashlight. The moon hadn't been full, but it had been bright. Could he have been so stubborn and defiant as to ignore such a clear warning?

"We can go back, ma'am, if you're ready," said Deputy Trujillo gently. He was standing beside Tony. I hadn't noticed his approach.

I looked at him, wanting to explain what I'd just understood, but unable to pinpoint its significance. It just *felt* important, maybe because it hadn't occurred to me before.

"I was just looking at that sign," I said.

Trujillo nodded. "Yeah, that's old Ezra's. His land's the other side of that fence."

"Is he the...the miner?"

Trujillo gave a soft laugh. "He'd like to be, if he could find something to mine. So far he's just been tearing up his land."

I looked back at the rockfall. Had it been caused by a human? If so, he was either very strong, or very persistent.

"There's no gold in these hills," said Milagro, still standing where he had sung. He looked up at the sky, then turned and started walking back toward the ranch.

We all followed.

By the time we got back it was past noon. Lunch would be underway in the dining hall. I was hungry, thirsty, and footsore, but immeasurably glad that I'd witnessed Milagro's singing. I thanked him, stumbling over my words of gratitude. He just nodded.

"You needed it too," he said.

His dark eyes held my gaze for a long moment. "Spirit friend," he said, so quietly I wasn't sure I'd heard him right. Then with a small smile he turned to talk to Trujillo.

I looked at Tony. Had he heard?

"Hungry?" he said.

I sighed. "Starving."

"Let's get lunch."

The dining hall was subdued. Of the football crowd, only Flag Hat Guy was present—sans hat, for once—at the far end of a table by the windows. There probably wasn't a game on; it was Monday, a holiday, at midday. Maybe the others were sleeping off the previous night's excitement.

Or maybe most of the weekend guests had left. This was a vacation spot after all. I'd almost forgotten that Tony and I were here on vacation. Ostensibly.

Lunch was burritos, with cornbread on the side and green chile stew at the soup station. I skipped the salad bar, promising myself I'd be more virtuous at dinner time. The Roans were not in the hall. Tony and I chose seats at the middle of a table near the fireplace. Though the fire had been allowed to die down, there was still some residual warmth, and the smell of pine logs burning.

"Has Mrs. Roan texted you?" Tony asked.

I checked my phone. "No. Why?"

"I need to talk to her."

What now? I thought it, but didn't say it.

Watching the comings and goings in the dining hall, I noted that some of the guests were heavily bundled in winter gear—they looked more like hunters than tourists—and wondered if they were camping. There was a campground on the ranch, though January didn't seem to me to be an ideal time.

I finished my cornbread, and considered getting another piece as I ate the last of my stew. Every time someone came out of the cafeteria line I looked up, hoping to see Lisette and Jeremy. No sign of them yet, but I did see Deputy Trujillo emerge from the line with a plate. He added a bowl of stew and a cup of coffee, then spied us and came over.

"Can I sit with you?" he asked.

"Sure," Tony said. I smiled and nodded.

Trujillo flashed me a grin as he sat across from me. Trusting for a cop; it placed him with his back to the room. Tony and I were side by side, facing the main entrance. Maybe Trujillo was counting on Tony to cover him.

"Got tired of those turkey sandwiches," he said, picking up his cornbread.

"Have you seen the Roans this morning?" Tony asked in a low voice. No other guests were near us.

Trujillo shook his head, chewed his mouthful, and swallowed. "I talked to her on the phone," he said quietly. "She doesn't know anything about a will."

Tony leaned back in his chair. "What about the lawyer?"

I gave him a questioning look.

"Lawyer was Roan's business manager," Trujillo explained to me, then he looked at Tony. "Talked to him, too. Far as he knows there's no will. He'd been trying to pin Roan down and get him to make one."

No will. Poor Lisette! Another mess to deal with.

"What will happen?" I asked.

"Texas law says the kid gets half, wife gets half," Tony said.

Well, it could be worse. I watched Tony and Trujillo, trying to get a read on them. Were they still suspicious of Lisette?

"Have you interviewed Flag Hat Guy?" I asked, glancing in his direction.

Trujillo gave me a confused look.

"Cartwright," Tony said. "Yes, they did. He's got an alibi—the football game. He and his buddies were in the cantina all evening. Jeremy confirmed that, so they can be grateful to him."

Damn. Who did that leave?

The cowboy trail guides. I didn't much care for them, especially Ted, but it really was unlikely that he'd have chosen to hang his victim where the tour guests might spot him. There was his partner's absence, but maybe there was an explanation there.

"Did you talk to any of the staff?" I asked. "The stable staff?"

"Yep," Trujillo said. "Talked to all of them. They were all in the Staff House Saturday night, playing poker."

Damn.

What if they had made a posse, and agreed to the poker story as a group alibi? No—that was too far-fetched. And as far as I knew there were hoofprints from only one horse at the scene of the hanging.

Regretfully, I abandoned the stable staff as suspects. Who was left? I thought back over the last couple of days, all the people I'd met or observed, trying to recall any anomalies. Lots of people had seemed annoyed by Wesley, but which ones had exhibited extreme behavior?

"Ezra," I said, thinking aloud.

Trujillo gave me an interested look. "Why? He never met Roan."

I shrugged. "He's so angry about protecting his land."

"That's just how he is," Trujillo said. "Been like that forever, but he's never done any harm. He's all bark, no bite. Worst I ever heard of was he fired his shotgun in the air at one of the ranch hands, and a couple of spent balls rained down on them."

"When was that?" Tony asked.

"Four, five years ago. He got hauled into court, ranted a little, paid his fine and that was that."

"No remorse?"

"I wasn't here at the time, but I think he convinced the judge he was sorry."

I frowned, thinking about Ezra. I'd seen him in Bode's Sunday afternoon, buying canned goods. Stocking up for the storm.

"How far away is his cabin?" I asked. "I heard the trail guides saying they hadn't seen him."

"That's not unusual," Trujillo said. "He's really a recluse. Comes out for a meal now and then, but mostly keeps to himself. I guess we could do a welfare check."

"You interviewed him about the crime?"

"Romero sent someone over and asked him to come in. Ezra cussed him for his trouble."

"But did he come?" Tony asked.

Trujillo looked as if he was just realizing he might have missed something important. "I'll have to check Romero's notes. I was out talking to ranch staff most of the day Saturday, after we spoke to you," Trujillo said, nodding to me.

"There's Lisette!" I said, as I saw her coming out of the cafeteria line with Jeremy. They headed for the soup station.

"I'll go check whether Ezra came in," Trujillo said, standing and picking up his plate. He stuffed the last of his cornbread in his mouth as he strode away.

I looked at Tony. Cop face; impassive.

OK. Trujillo must be leaving it to us to talk to Lisette. He and Tony must have agreed to that. Was Tony counting on my friendship with Lisette to get her to be more open?

Well, if he was, I intended to help her show him her innocence.

Having served herself a bowl of stew, Lisette turned and scanned the room. I gave a small wave when her gaze crossed mine, and she smiled, then headed our way with Jeremy following.

"I'll get us some coffee," Tony said, standing. "Cream and sugar?"

"Just cream," I said.

The Roans made their way over to our table. "Hi," I said as they arrived.

Lisette took the chair Trujillo had vacated. Her shiner was already less noticeable. Besides the chile stew she had a plate of salad and a piece of cornbread.

Tony returned with the coffee, nodded to Lisette, then sat down and kept his eyes on his plate, methodically cutting small bites of his burrito. Trying to be invisible, I thought.

Jeremy's plate held two burritos, which he had smothered in red and green chile sauce from the condiments table. Having tried some of both with my own burrito, I knew that they were pretty spicy. His drink, I noted, was a large glass of soda.

"Wow, that's a lot of chile," I said. "Did you taste it?"

"It's Christmas!" Jeremy said, picking up his knife and fork.

Lisette looked at me. "He saw one of the ranch hands doing it that way," she said. "That's what they called it: Christmas."

"Red and green," Tony said, without looking up.

"Do you like spicy food?" I asked, but Jeremy had already taken a large bite. As I watched, his eyes widened, and he hastily gave his mouthful a couple of chews, then swallowed and reached for his soda.

"You might not want to—" I began.

"Aaaaahh!" Jeremy said after one pull at the soda.

I jumped up and dashed to the coffee and tea station, grabbed a pint of milk from the refrigerator, and hurried back. "Drink this," I said, handing the milk to Jeremy, who was fanning his open mouth with his hands.

He took a big swig, and after a few seconds calmed down. Gasping (a trifle dramatically), he continued to drink the milk until it was gone. Lisette quietly set his plate aside, and when he'd finished his milk, offered him her cornbread. He accepted this, and nibbled at it.

"Thank you," Lisette said to me.

I smiled ruefully. "Sorry I wasn't quicker."

"It's OK." She looked at her son. "Now he knows to taste things before taking a lot of them."

Tony coughed, and took a deep pull at his coffee. I glanced at him, suspicious, but if he was concealing amusement he did it very well. He caught me looking, finished the last of his burrito in one larger-than-usual bite, and stood.

"Be right back," he said, picking up his empty plate and heading toward the kitchen. He grabbed Jeremy's burritos on his way.

I looked at Lisette. "I hope your morning wasn't too awful."

She shrugged. "It's going to be awful for a while," she said softly.

Jeremy looked up at her with sad eyes. She put an arm around him for a shoulder hug.

"Feeling better?" she asked him.

He nodded, and took another small bite of cornbread. Lisette smiled at him, a sad smile, but not a broken one. This horrible weekend, I realized, was the beginning of a better life for them. I didn't want to think about what life with Wesley had been like. I'd seen more than enough to know it had been unhappy and probably frightening. Life without him might be challenging, but it would be better.

"Did you do something fun this morning?" Lisette asked me.

"Ah—" I said, wondering how to describe the excursion with Trujillo and Bernardo Milagro. Deciding it was better not to, I simply said, "We went for a walk in the snow."

Lisette nodded, and flashed a small smile. "It's beautiful. I'd love to paint it."

"You could sketch it," I suggested gently.

She met my gaze, and for a moment her chin trembled, then she took a breath. "Yes," she said. "I think I will."

Tony returned, carrying a plate with two pieces of cornbread, and a wrapped ice cream bar. He set the plate beside Lisette, and handed the ice cream to Jeremy, who commenced tearing it open at once.

"Where'd you find that?" I asked. "I didn't see them."

"I asked one of the cooks if they had any ice cream."

"That was kind of you," Lisette said. "Thank you."

Tony smiled. *"De nada."*

"What do you say?" Lisette said to Jeremy.

He paused in destroying the wrapper to look up at Tony. "Thank you," he said meekly.

"You're welcome," Tony told him. He picked up his mug. "Anyone want coffee?"

Lisette's head rose, then she glanced at me.

"I'm fine," I said, lifting my mostly-full mug. My coffee was lukewarm, but that was all right.

Lisette looked at Tony. "Yes, please."

"How do you like it?" Tony asked.

"Black."

As will sometimes happen, the word rang out into a moment of silence in the hall. Lisette looked flustered and frozen simultaneously, like a deer in the headlights. Tony nodded and went away to the coffee stand.

"Do you have a favorite painting of O'Keeffe's?" I asked Lisette, to fill the silence.

She gave me a grateful look, and nodded. "I've always liked *New York with Moon,* because it reminds me of New Orleans, but I think my favorite is *From the Plains I.* What about you?"

"A favorite? I'm not sure...so many of them are wonderful. I adore the datura paintings. I think she called them jimson weed."

"Like the one she did for Elizabeth Arden?"

"Yes. But I think...actually, my favorite may be *Black Place III.*" I lowered my voice a little, to avoid another awkward moment.

Lisette gave me a long, steady look, then nodded. "Yes. I like that one, too. It resonates with so many different things. Did you notice that the gray and red hills around here are like the ones at the bottom of that painting?"

"No!" I tried to remember the painting, but that detail had not leapt out at me. "I know the hills you mean, though. There's more of that formation just to the east. Now I want to look at the painting!"

"I've got a picture of it in a book in my room, if you want to come see," Lisette said.

"Thanks, I'd like that."

Tony returned with a mug of coffee for Lisette, and sat beside me with his own mug. Lisette gave him a brief smile.

"Thank you."

Tony nodded, then raised his head, looking past her. I followed his gaze and saw Flag Hat Guy approaching.

Now *I* felt like a deer in the headlights. What could he want?

My heart started racing with fear for Lisette's safety. I tried to tell myself it was irrational, but there was a chance it wasn't. What could I do to protect her, if need be? Throw my coffee in his face?

But Tony was here. Tony would take care of us. I sensed his readiness.

"Ma'am?"

Flag Hat had come around to stand by the empty chair next to Lisette. She looked up at him, rather haughtily.

"I just wanted to say I'm sorry about your husband."

Lisette's face was a formal mask. She blinked once, and a swallow moved her throat.

Flag Hat shoved a hand in his pocket. Next to me, Tony stiffened. The hand came out holding a wallet, and I was able to breathe again.

Flag Hat pulled a wad of cash out of the wallet and put it on the table next to Lisette's plate. "I won this off your husband in a bet," he said. "I want you to have it."

It was twenties. There had to be at least five hundred dollars in that stack, I thought.

Lisette's gaze was fixed on the money. "Keep it," she said finally. "You won it fair and square."

"I did," Flag Hat said, "but I don't feel right keeping it, after what happened."

"Then donate it to the ranch," Lisette said.

Silence. No one moved for a long moment, then, "All right, I will," said Flag Hat Guy quietly. He picked up the money but did not return it to his wallet. "I'm sorry for your loss, ma'am," he said, and his other hand went to his brow, where the brim of his hat would have been. He glanced at me and Tony, then quietly walked away, toward the west doors to the hall, where there was a donation box.

Lisette closed her eyes, her brow drawn into a furrow of grief. Jeremy watched her with anxious eyes. Tony and I remained silent. I glanced up in time to see Flag Hat stuff the money into the donation box before leaving the building.

"You OK?" Tony asked softly. He was talking to Lisette.

She opened her eyes to look at him, swallowed again, then nodded.

"Shall we give you some space?" I asked.

"No, please stay."

Jeremy leaned over to whisper to his mother. She nodded, and he got up. I watched him head for the restroom.

Lisette took a sip of coffee, then looked at Tony. "I'd like to leave today," she said, a note of challenge in her voice.

"We're still trying to locate a will. Can you think of anyplace Mr. Roan might have stashed one?"

"Wesley didn't write a will," she said.

"How can you be sure?" Tony asked. "He might not have told you about it."

She fixed him with a hard stare, then picked up her mug with a sigh. "Wesley couldn't read."

12

"Couldn't *read*?" I echoed, astonished.

Lisette nodded. "He was illiterate. He could recognize a few words, could sign his name, but..." She shook her head. "I paid all the bills, ran the household, talked to the business manager. And I read every contract before I let him sign it," she added fiercely.

My mind went back to the arroyo, to a flash of blue and white. "My God. Tony, he couldn't *read!* He wouldn't have understood that warning sign! What if he left the arroyo and stumbled into those rocks in the dark? He could have fallen...."

Tony's head rose sharply. He stared into the distance for a second, then stood. "Please excuse me, ma'am." He pulled his phone out and was talking before he reached the door.

Lisette looked at me, eyes full of questions. "What warning sign?" she asked finally, just as Jeremy returned.

I looked at Wesley's son, who would have better opportunities than his father. Looked at Lisette, unsure how much I should tell her, how much she knew. Looked at my coffee, stone cold now.

"Let's go for a walk," I said.

We left by the west doors and headed up the road, which curved north past the cantina and another building with a playground. To our left was a mesa, perhaps fifty feet higher than the rest of the ranch, though that might be enough to give it glorious views. I remembered seeing it marked on the trail map. There was lodging up there, more of the dormitory-style buildings. From here, the way up was by steep little switchback trails, and in consideration of Lisette's footwear, I stayed on the road.

It was sloppy in the melting snow; it needed a new course of gravel. I walked slowly, for Lisette's sake. Jeremy had no trouble keeping up. I noted he was wearing his ear-buds. Occasionally he would gesture or dance a step to the rhythm only he could hear. Escaping into music. I had done that myself, many times.

I wondered if Tony and Trujillo would be able to find evidence of Wesley among the rocks. If my suspicion was right, he had fallen and hit his head on one of the boulders that were jumbled behind the fence. And the sign had said "unstable"—maybe he'd lost his footing on loose rock. Would the snow mask any sign of him?

My mind followed Wesley on his last, disastrous journey. Having battered his wife, he took off running, away from the last semblance of civilization on the ranch. Running down a moonlit road, running from the anger.

Running from himself? From his own pain, from his own inadequacy?

No wonder he was angry at the world. The world had secret knowledge that, for whatever reason, had been denied him. And probably he felt taunted by it every day of his life.

His wife had the secret knowledge. His *son* had it. Everyone but him.

And in the end, his lack of that knowledge had killed him.

Lisette stopped. We had come to a fork in the road. The left branch angled northwest, hugging the mesa. The other continued north. Lisette stood gazing at the cliffs before us. The sun had melted all the snow off their faces, and the sky was once again a backdrop of glowing blue. With just a sugar-frosting of snow along the top of the ridge, it was gorgeous.

"There's that gray and red," Lisette said, pointing. Just beyond the ridgeline of the mesa, the red foothills were visible, striped with silver-gray as they rose to the base of the cliffs.

I watched her take it in. Committing the colors and the shapes to memory, perhaps, or maybe just breathing in the feeling of the place. I stood still, while Jeremy bopped around us to the music only he could hear. Silence was what I heard: silence, and the whisper of the wind among the rocks, among the small trees. I inhaled a deep breath of snow-and-pine-scented air.

Lisette turned to me. "Tell me."

"I don't know how much you already know," I said, reluctant to cause her more pain.

"Just tell me everything."

So I did. Starting with the trail ride, and finding Wesley's body, and the sign I saw later. I told her what I knew by my own observation, and not what Tony or Trujillo had told me. It was enough; Lisette frowned as I described the rockfall, the poor fence between it and the arroyo, and Ezra's sign.

"So you think his death was an accident?" she said.

"It may have been." I coughed. "Did they give you the autopsy results?"

"They offered to. I haven't had time, or…the heart."

"The rope didn't kill him," I said. "He was already dead."

Lisette gaped at me. "Then who strung him up in the tree?"

"I'm not sure, but it may have been the old man who owns the land beyond the fence. He definitely doesn't like anyone coming on his land."

"But, *why?*"

I gave a shrug. "All I can think of is maybe he found Wesley and wanted him off his land, so he tried to make it look like someone had hanged him."

"That's crazy!"

"It is, kind of. Yeah."

Crazy and sad. Very sad.

Jeremy had stopped bopping, and stood watching his mother. She glanced at him, and sighed.

"Let's go back. It's cold."

I turned, then froze. "Don't move," I whispered.

Looking over my shoulder, I saw that the Roans had obeyed. I nodded my head toward the side of the mesa a few yards south of us. A doe stood there, head up, ears wide, watching us. After a few seconds, it turned and strolled up the hill, catching up with two other deer.

We watched in silence until they disappeared over the mesa top.

"See?" Lisette murmured. "I told you."

Jeremy's face glowed with delight. "That was *cool!*"

I smiled, then looked at Lisette. "Tea?"

"Yes."

I broke out the Lapsang Souchong. It seemed right for the occasion. I had milk and sugar, and Lisette accepted both, for once. We sat in the Room of Many Chairs, sipping mugs of the strong, smoky brew with an underlying tang of pine. I wished the fireplace wasn't blocked; a fire would have been nice.

Jeremy was lost in his phone, earbuds in, thumbs flying. I watched him for a while, then looked at Lisette.

"I assume Jeremy has no trouble reading," I said quietly.

She met my gaze. "He's an A student, despite what you see. He's quite sharp, and Auntie Rachelle knows just how to bribe him to do his homework even if he's bored with it."

I nodded, feeling a desire to meet Auntie Rachelle. They'd be all right, this family.

From the other room came strains of Mozart: my phone's ring-tone. I glanced at Lisette.

"I'm sorry—"

"Answer it," she said. "It might be your man."

I put down my mug and went to get the phone. It was indeed Tony.

"You were right," he said. "We found Roan's blood on one of the boulders."

"How? Weren't they covered with snow?"

"Yeah. Trujillo brought in a bloodhound. Went right to it."

"Oh!"

"Dog's trainer almost broke a leg. That rockslide is loose. Trujillo thinks Ezra made it, digging in the hillsides."

"Did he ever come in?"

"No. We're going to go check on him now."

I pictured the two of them knocking on the door of a cabin. Inside, one terrified, cranky old man with a shotgun. I wished they could send an interceptor instead.

"Please be careful," I said.

"Babe, I'm always careful. Don't worry. Call you when we're done."

"May I tell Lisette?"

"Yeah, go ahead."

Dead air. He'd hung up. I put down the phone and returned to Lisette, who was watching me intently.

"It was an accident. Wesley fell and hit his head on a boulder. They found his blood."

She let out her breath in a sharp sigh, looked at the ceiling, then buried her face in her hands. She took a shuddering breath, and sobbed once.

Nothing had changed, really. There was still hate in the world, and the kind of hate that had made Lisette—and me—fear, and even expect the worst, was easy to find. But the fact that in this case, in Wesley's death, that hate had not played a part, was a source of enormous relief.

Jeremy took out his earbuds and laid them with his phone on the chair next to his, then stood and went over to Lisette. "Momma?" he said.

She lifted her head, then wrapped him in her arms. He hugged her back.

I decided it was time to refill the kettle.

Lisette's phone rang not long after Tony called me. She answered it, had a brief conversation, then left with Jeremy. I busied myself with tidying up the tea things, and then with packing. Theoretically we were leaving today. I sighed as I carefully rolled up my nice dress and tucked it into my suitcase. Our fancy-dinner money would probably end up paying for an extra day's lodging. I put the unopened wine and the souvenir mug in with my tea things, carefully folded the dragonfly necklace in tissue and tucked it into my little jewelry case, then wrapped the jade plant back up in its paper cocoon and nestled it in the top of the bag.

Out of things to do, I tried to read, but couldn't focus. It wasn't until Tony called again that I was able to relax.

"Nobody got shot," were his first words.

"I'm glad to hear it. Was Ezra at home?"

"Yep. Acted mad, but was actually scared—um, out of his mind. Had to talk him down off the ceiling."

"Did he admit to..." I couldn't say it.

"Yeah, eventually. He didn't know Roan was dead when he shot him. Then he was scared that he'd killed him, and mad at him for trespassing at the same time. He didn't think things through, just wanted to get rid of the body, so he got his horse and dragged it over to the tree."

I swallowed, sad and horrified.

"Trujillo took him down to the station in Española to give a statement," Tony added.

"What will happen to him?"

"Don't know. If they decide to order an evaluation, he could end up in an institution. He's pretty incoherent. Or if things go badly—if the judge is unsympathetic, he might do a little time."

I winced. Prison would not be kind to a man like Ezra. "Does he have any family?"

"Not around here, I don't think."

"How sad."

"Yeah. Listen, we have a couple of loose ends to tie up, then I'll be ready to head home. Is Mrs. Roan there with you?"

"No, she left a while ago."

"OK. Be there soon."

Silence.

I put the phone in my purse, ready to go. Remembering that I still had the mug I'd borrowed from the cafeteria, I stepped into the Room of Many Chairs to fetch it. The light coming in through the windows was getting dim. Tony had been gone all afternoon; the day was nearly over.

I was ready for a change from cafeteria food. If Tony didn't want to stop at the Abiquiu Inn, I'd lobby for a burger in Española on the way home. Meanwhile, I put on my coat and walked over to the dining hall to return the mug.

People were waiting in line outside the cafeteria door. I went in the west doors and took the mug to the dishwashing station. Much clattering of pans issued from the kitchen, and there was a fresh-baked bread smell that made my stomach growl. I considered getting a carry-out cup of coffee to tide me over. Actually, mocha, I decided, eyeing the cocoa packets near the tea bags.

While I was concocting my beverage, Ted the trail guide and his partner came over to the coffee machine.

"—took him into town, is what Stacey said."

"Eee, they're gonna jail him!"

"Can't believe old Ezra would up and kill a guy."

I struggled, because in fact Ezra had been willing to shoot a guy he didn't know was dead. But the truth was more important than nit-picking details.

"He didn't," I said, stirring my mocha.

"Huh?" Ted looked at me in surprise.

"If you're talking about Wesley Roan," I said, "his death was apparently an accident. He fell and hit his head on a boulder."

"How do you know?" asked Ted.

I gave him a look. Had he forgotten my finding the body, and Tony's response?

"My fiancé's been helping with the investigation."

I hoped, belatedly, that Tony wouldn't be annoyed by my telling the guides it was an accident. Maybe a district attorney somewhere would be disappointed at that word getting out, but oh, well. I put a lid on my cup and started for the doors.

"Hey, wait a sec," Ted called. "Does Ezra have a lawyer?"

I turned back. "I have no idea. If he doesn't, he'll surely be assigned one, if it goes to court."

Ted frowned, then turned to his buddy. "We need to go find him. If he needs a lawyer, we'll get him one."

I blinked, trying to picture these two even conversing with a lawyer. That was unfair, I supposed. There were cowboyish lawyers in this state.

"He's your friend, then?" I said.

"Hell, no. He's a cranky old pain in the ass," Ted said. "Beg pardon."

His partner nodded, then looked at me. "But he's our neighbor," he added.

I smiled. Maybe Ezra wasn't so alone after all.

"You'll want to talk to Deputy Trujillo," I said. "Make sure you find him, don't just talk to Sheriff Romero."

"Huh. Romero," scoffed Ted. "Thanks, we will."

I headed out into the evening. It was dusk. The cafeteria line was moving now. As I crossed the road, I saw more movement: the deer were back, pawing away the slush to nibble on the grass in front of the Library. I counted four—then six, eight, twelve. They blithely ignored me as I turned down the road toward the Ghost House.

A chill breeze rose up, making me glad for the mocha. I sipped it as I picked my way through the melting snow, avoiding patches where it had gone to slush or mud. Judging by the chill, it would soon be frozen again.

The two giant cottonwoods stood guard over the Ghost House,

their branches reaching high into the night sky. I paused to look up at them. The lowest branches had to be twenty feet off the ground—far too high for a hanging. A hundred years ago there must have been lower branches.

I gazed up at them, pale against the gloaming, gently swaying in the breeze. Easy to imagine the whisper of voices in the grating of the highest branches. I listened, but heard only the cold sigh of the wind among the leafless boughs. My ears were getting cold.

Then, faint and distant, a woman's voice: "Ellen!"

My back muscles tightened, then I looked around. Up the hill, toward the other casitas, a light was bobbing. I waited, sipping my mocha, until it moved closer and resolved into Lisette, carrying a flashlight.

"Hi," I said. "Where's Jeremy?"

"Packing," she said, slightly out of breath. "We're leaving."

"Tonight?"

"Soon as I can get him in the car. I'm ready to shake off the dust of this place!"

"Or the mud," I said.

She laughed. "I wanted to say goodbye, and thank you for all your help and support."

I moved toward the door to my room. "Come on in for a minute. It's cold."

"OK, but just for a minute. No tea!"

"Aw, you make me sound like a pusher."

"You *are* a pusher!"

We stamped our feet on the doormat and went in. The room was blissfully warm. In the light, I saw that Lisette's quilted, tailored coat was a deep shade of purple. Her face was calm, if a bit tired.

I set down my cup and went to my tea-gear bag, carefully extracting the O'Keeffe biography, which I handed to her. "I want you to have this. I think you'll enjoy it."

"But you're not finished," she said, fingering my bookmark.

"I almost am. I can get it from the library for the last chapter."

"Thank you." Lisette smiled, then reached out and gathered me into a hug. "Thank you for everything! I don't know what I would have done if you hadn't been here."

I hugged her back. "Where are you staying next?"

"Santa Fe, just for the night. We head home tomorrow."

"You've got my card. Please stay in touch."

"I will. And we'll be back another time to see Santa Fe. I have to visit the O'Keeffe Museum, and I want to have tea at your place!"

I smiled. "I hope you'll let me join you."

"Sure thing!"

The sound of the door unlocking made us turn. Tony came in, then checked when he saw Lisette.

"Sorry," he said. "Didn't know you had company."

"I'm just leaving," Lisette said, then paused and drew herself up, becoming formal, the book tucked under one arm. "I'm grateful to you, Detective."

"Tony," he said. "Glad I could help."

Lisette looked from him to me. "When is your wedding?"

"In the fall," I said, wondering if she wanted an invitation.

She nodded. "I wish you a joyful marriage," she said with a fleeting smile, then moved to the door. "Goodbye."

"Bye," I said as she went out, pulling the door closed behind her.

A kind wish. How sad that her own marriage had been so lacking in joy. I turned to Tony, wanting a hug.

"Is it over?" I asked, muffled in his embrace.

"All but the paperwork. Fortunately, that's not my job."

"Sorry if I screwed anything up."

He held me at arm's length, eyes concerned. "You didn't. Why are you worried?"

I shrugged. "Well, I don't know all the rules. I did tell the stable guys that Wesley's death was an accident, just now."

"Well, it was."

"But I didn't know if it was OK to say so."

"Babe, don't overthink it. You did good." He kissed my forehead. "Ready to go?"

"As soon as you are."

Tony's packing consisted of throwing/cramming his clothing into his bag, and (at my insistence) putting his muddy cowboy boots in a shopping bag so as not to mess up the trunk of my car. It took less than five minutes, though I did have to remind him to pack his toothbrush. A final check of all the drawers, and we carried our bags out to the Camry.

Because of the snow, we elected to walk down the road to the parking lot in order to get to the welcome center. Climbing up all the steps, I remembered our arrival. It seemed an age ago, and it also felt like we hadn't really had a vacation. Tony must have felt that even more strongly. At least it had been a change of scene, I reflected. The hiking was good, and the scenery unquestionably gorgeous.

Debbie was behind the counter, and swiftly settled our bill. I glanced at it, confirming she hadn't charged us for an extra day.

"Thanks," I said, smiling.

She glanced at me, then at Tony. "Thank *you*," she said. "Victor says you both were a big help."

"Happy to," Tony said.

I glanced at the trading post, but decided I didn't need a memento. I had the mug, and Tony and I had the dragonfly necklace from Milagro. If I ever wanted anything else, Ghost Ranch was a short drive away.

Halfway down the steps, I paused. Away from the welcome center's lights, the snow was lit with soft moonglow. Looking up, I saw the moon riding high, just past half full. This was a beautiful place, magical even, but I wasn't sure I wanted to come back. Certainly not any time soon.

Tony's arm slid around me. "It was a good weekend," he said.

"Yeah."

"Except for the dead body."

I gave an exasperated laugh. "They follow me everywhere."

He chuckled and drew me in for a kiss. "My little corpse-magnet."

I'd have whapped him, but I didn't want to lose my balance on the steps. We picked our way back down to the parking lot, and walked back to the Ghost House.

There was no longer any question in my mind about whether Ghost Ranch would be a good place to get married. I definitely did *not* want to hold the wedding in a place where I'd discovered a body.

"Would you mind if we ate at the Abiquiu Inn?" I asked as we got in the car. "It's closest."

"Mind? I'm counting on it! We've been waiting for that all weekend."

I smiled. "Good."

"Besides, we deserve a reward."

"That we do," I agreed.

"I'm thinking margarita," Tony said.

"Oooh." I'd been thinking wine, myself, but a margarita sounded good.

I backed out and drove carefully down the road, feeling the tires slip just a little in the slush. When we got to the highway I breathed a sigh of relief as I turned onto the pavement, which had been plowed and generously sanded.

Visiting O'Keeffe's stark landscape had definitely been a change of pace, but there was a lot to be said for creature comforts. With a last glance at the moon shining down on the cow-skull gate, I headed back toward civilization.

Ellen's Lapsang Souchong with Cherry

Lapsang Souchong is a pine-smoked tea from Fujian Province. It is often a component of Russian Caravan blends, which are so named because tea first came to Russia by camel caravan from China.

A traditional way of serving Russian Caravan is with a spoonful of cherry preserve, often presented in a glass cup so the cherry may be admired. Ellen has borrowed this custom for Lapsang Souchong.

Ingredients:

Lapsang Souchong loose leaf tea
boiling water

Amarena cherries

Preparation:

Brew the tea. Fill a teacup (roughly 6 ounces). Add a couple of cherries and a teaspoon of syrup. Don't stir! Let the cherry flavor rise up through the tea as you drink it.

Serve with homemade marzipan or shortbread.

Tony's Augmentation:

Add ½ shot of single malt whiskey.

Wisteria Tearoom

upper floor

←N—

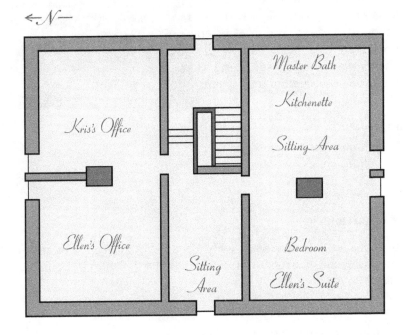

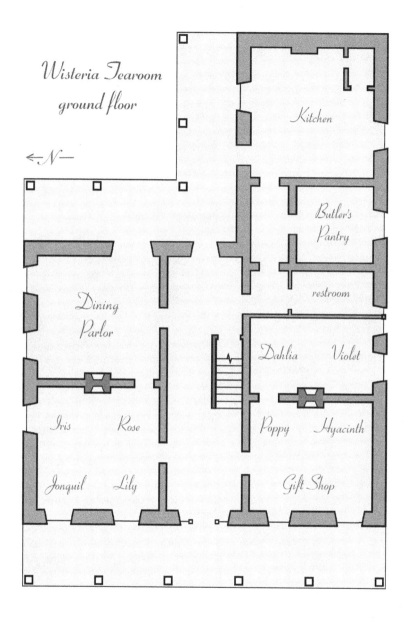

Wisteria Tearoom
ground floor

← N —

Kitchen

Butler's
Pantry

restroom

Dining
Parlor

Dahlia   Violet

Iris   Rose

Poppy   Hyacinth

Jonquil   Lily

Gift Shop

Wisteria Tearoom Staff

Ellen Rosings	Owner
Kris Overland	Office Manager
Julio Delgado	Chef
Mai Hanh	Assistant Chef
Ramon Garcia	Assistant
Mick Gallagher	Dish Washer
Dee Gallagher	Server
Rosa Garcia	Server
Iz Naranjo	Server
Dale Whittier	Server

Ellen's Family

Joe Rosings	Brother
Nat Salazar	Aunt
Manny Salazar	Uncle

Ellen's Friends & Associates

Gina Fiorello	Bestie
Tony Aragón	Fiancé
Willow Lane	Spirit Tour Guide

Tony's Family

Angela Aragón	Sister
Dolores Aragón	Mother
"*Abuela*" Aragón	Grandmother

About the Author

photo by Chris Krohn

PATRICE GREENWOOD was born and raised in New Mexico, and remembers when the Santa Fe Plaza was home to more dusty dogs than trendy art galleries. She has been writing fiction longer than she cares to admit, perpetrating over twenty published novels in various genres. She uses a different name for each genre, thus enabling her to pretend she is a Secret Agent.

She loves afternoon tea, old buildings, gourmet tailgating at the opera, ghost stories, costumes, and solving puzzles. Her popular Wisteria Tearoom Mysteries are colored by many of these interests. She is presently collapsed on her chaise longue, sipping Wisteria White tea and planning the next book in the series.